CW00500157

THE BOOK SWAP

JE ROWNEY

Happy Christmas
Claire!
Love,
J Rowney
xx

LITTLE FOX
PUBLISHING

Other thrillers by this author

Other People's Lives
I Can't Sleep
The Woman in the Woods

Be the first to hear about new releases by signing up to the author's mailing list. Visit http://jerowney.com for details.

If you enjoy reading this book, please remember to leave a review. Reviews help readers find new books and help authors to find new readers.

This is a work of fiction. Names, characters, business, events and incidents are the products of the author's imagination. Any resemblance to actual persons, living or dead, or actual events is purely coincidental. Where the names of actual persons are used in this book, the characters themselves are entirely fictional and are not intended to bear any resemblance to persons with those names.

All rights reserved.

© JE Rowney and Little Fox Publishing, 2022

For Becky Sumner,
who suggested including
Book Swap Central in a novel.

CHAPTER ONE

Laura lifted her mug to her lips and took a sip of her coffee. Moments later, the cold brown liquid came spluttering back out, narrowly missing the book, but landing on the arm of her mother's armchair. She had let it go cold again.

"How many times?" she asked, but the only person to hear her words was herself.

Laura's life had changed dramatically over the previous few months. Separating from her husband and moving back with her mother for the first time since she had moved out to get married, she barely had any time to herself. Sitting down to read had become a luxury, but every time she managed to curl up for a few chapters, she found herself forgetting the rest of the world, which unfortunately included the coffee she had made to accompany her book break.

"Did you say something, love?"

Laura's mother, Catharine, peered into the living room.

"No, I'm fine," Laura said, moving her book to cover the small brown patch. "Thanks, Mum."

Her mother stood in the doorway, casting her eyes over her, as though trying to work out whether she was telling the truth.

"You can talk to me, you know," she said, without moving closer.

"I know, Mum." Laura shifted in her chair. Either she had been sitting in the same position for too long or she felt the pressure of her mother's concern boring into her. It had been four months, and if she hadn't talked to her mum about the breakdown of her marriage by then, she wasn't likely to start.

Sensing the barrier between them rising, Catharine didn't push further.

"How's the book?" she asked instead.

"Uh, it's okay. I'll lend it to you when I've finished."

"One of those thrillers, is it?"

Catharine took her chance to come into the room and walk over to her daughter, peering at the book cover. The tell-tale imagery of a psychological thriller, a yellow-windowed house in ominous darkness, was emblazoned across the front.

"Yeah," Laura said.

It wasn't just that she didn't want to talk about her failed marriage, Laura didn't want to talk at all. Since leaving her husband, it was almost as though she had clammed up and closed herself off from everyone she knew. Including her mum.

Aware of the snappiness of her response, she added, "It was one of those I got from that book swap. You know, that group I'm in."

"On the World Wide Web?" Catharine pronounced each word carefully, as though it tasted strange in her mouth.

"Facebook, yeah," Laura replied.

Catharine nodded.

"That's nice, love."

Laura couldn't help but think that her mother would consider any social interaction she had was 'nice'. She had stayed in the house, not answering the phone to her friends, taking time out of work, all under the guise of healing and getting over her broken marriage.

Social media was easy, though. She could talk to the people that lived in her phone, on the Facebook app. Her one true love had always been reading, and –

unlike her soon to be ex-husband – it would never leave her.

Being in a group with thousands of other like-minded people from around the world was all the community she needed. She didn't have to talk about why she had split from the man she had planned to spend her life with. Nobody needed to know why she still didn't feel like she could return to work after almost five months. There were no intrusive questions, and nobody was judging her for being a thirty-year-old woman that lived with her mum.

The group chatted about books they were reading, books they had loved, books that had driven them crazy. Books, books, books. Laura loved it.

"What happened there?" Catharine leaned over her daughter, investigating the splash of tan brown liquid on her cream armchair.

Even though she was a grown woman, Laura couldn't help but feel like a child when she had done something wrong.

"Sorry, Mum," she said. "I was going to come and …"

But Catharine was already reaching down, wiping away at the mark, humming away to herself.

It seemed like she always had a cloth in her hand since Laura came home. Everything was in perfect order. The carpet hoovered twice a day, washing up, never sitting, waiting to be done, clean dishes dried and put away as soon as they were washed. Heavens forbid Laura left the towels out of place in the bathroom.

"Leave it. I'll do it." Laura put her book down on the carved oak end table that had sat by the sofa since the days that her father was still alive. "Mum …"

"All done," Catharine said. "Try to be more careful though, love."

"I didn't mean to do it." Laura could already feel herself becoming defensive. The sharp edge her husband had always hated entered her voice and made her wince.

Catherine placed her hand, gently, onto Laura's arm.

"I know," she said, her voice as soft as Laura's was hard. "Why don't I make you a fresh brew, and you can get another chapter in while I finish in the kitchen?"

Laura didn't resist the warmth in her mum's voice or the touch of her hand. No matter what, she knew that Catharine only had good intentions. It was difficult, sometimes, not to overreact or lash out. Her temperament had not yet settled after her split.

"Thanks. And I'm sorry. About the …" she pointed at the splash mark that was now so faint that it was barely visible.

Catharine shook her head and smiled.

"Go on now, get stuck back in. I'll never get to read it if you don't finish."

Eleven o'clock in the morning, a time when once the confident and seemingly happily married Laura Jacobs would be sitting at her desk in the office of Chaucer and Sons. A couple of hours of paperwork, then perhaps a visit out to show a prospective buyer around a property. Once she had a purpose, places to be, people to see. Now mornings were for coffee and books. Catharine would make lunch and then encourage her daughter to take a walk with her in the afternoons. Then evenings were either filled with television marathons or, commonly, more reading. With her head in a book, Laura was in her own world, and sometimes even her own universe.

All the drama in her life was fictional, and Laura liked it that way.

Little did she know that things were about to change.

Tucking her legs beneath her on the large, soft armchair, Laura leaned back and started to read.

She devoured one page, and then the next. By the time she had reached the third, the outside world had ceased to exist. There was nothing apart from the world the author had created within the pages of the book.

Reading was her escape. The world within the book may have been filled with drama, danger, and deceit, but it was a different world, a world where she didn't have to think about the drama, danger, and deceit of her own life.

A shrill ringing from the hallway broke Laura's concentration and dragged her back from her novel into her less desirable reality.

In her marital home, she had insisted that she and Jamie had a doorbell that chimed gently, after suffering the harsh trill of her parents' ringer for so many years. All those things she had argued for had been left behind. None of them mattered anymore. She wondered whether they ever had at all.

"I'll get it," Catharine called from the kitchen. Laura could tell by the shift in tone that she was already walking, heading to the door.

"Thanks."

No point carrying on reading for the time being. Laura pulled her phone from her pocket and scrolled through social media.

She heard the click of the heavy wooden door opening, and then the familiar sound of the voice that her mother used with strangers. It was a lighter, more honey-sweet tone than her usual sound, and the two of them often laughed about it. How easy it could be to disguise one's feelings just by changing one's voice. Laura had been doing the same thing ever since she split from Jamie.

There was a second click as her mother closed the door. Only then did Laura speak.

"Who was it?" Laura called through into the hall.

"Parcel for you," her mum said, rather unnecessarily as she walked in holding a padded envelope. "Expecting something? Feels rather like a book, I'd say."

Laura's mood lifted as soon as she saw the delivery.

"Thanks, Mum." She reached up for the package and read her name and her mother's address on the parcel.

One good thing about living here instead of living with her husband was that she was no longer judged for her book mail. Jamie had complained every time he saw the postman arrive. He didn't understand Laura's passion for reading.

"Probably because he's never picked up a book himself," Catharine would always say.

The parcel was wrapped in brown paper, her name danced in green marker pen. Someone had taken the time to pick this book out for her from their own bookshelf. They had wrapped it carefully and handwritten her name on the crisp packaging. Before she had even opened the parcel, Laura was already buzzing with excitement.

"Are you going to open it now?" Catharine asked.

Laura set the package down on her dad's table.

"I'll save it," she said. "I'll be done with this one today, then I can open the parcel and dive straight in."

She took one last look at the freshly arrived mail, smiled to herself, and settled back to finish her book.

CHAPTER TWO

The following day was much like every other day had been since Laura had moved in with her mum. After reading and half-watching the daytime television shows that her mother couldn't stop watching, Laura took herself out into the garden to sit in the little outhouse that had once been her father's tool shed. After he died, it sat unused for almost three years, before her mother finally brought herself to sort through the contents.

There was so much inside that he had gathered over the years. Nothing of financial value to anyone, but the sentimental value was immeasurable. Of course, there were actual tools, but there were also gadgets that he had tinkered away at, sketches of intricate objects that he would never get to complete, even handwritten notes that he had made about future projects or plans that he never had time to work on.

Jonathan Deacon had been a practical man, who loved nothing more than creating and repairing. The shed had been his domain, his sacred ground. It was little wonder that Catharine had not wanted to disturb it.

Still, time passed, and the pain of loss never left, but it lessened. The shed became Catharine's place for time alone as she sifted through the stacks, picked through boxes, and separated Jonathan's belongings into what she would keep and what she could let go of. And again, later, a second pass, where she whittled down the ten boxes of memories into just two. The essence of her husband, Laura's father, decanted into cardboard storage containers, to be kept for eternity.

Then came the transformation of the sacred space into the garden room that stood to the present day. Wooden slats were removed and replaced with windows, the dirty workbench and vice switched for a neat desk, Jonathan's sturdy chair made way for a deep, comfortable sofa. Laura covered her clothes in white overalls to help her mother paint over the rough walls with eggshell paints, and one of Jonathan's friends came to lay floorboards over the concrete ground.

When the work was completed, and the shed was transformed into somewhere the women could sit, relax and remember the man who had been such an important, beloved part of their lives, the finishing touch was placed. In almost ceremonial fashion, Catharine set a framed photograph of the three of them onto the newly fitted desk. The last holiday they had taken together, before Jonathan's diagnosis. That was how Laura wanted to remember him, how she wanted to remember her family. Close, happy, healthy.

Now, most days, she would sit in the garden room that had once been his universe, relaxing and reflecting. No matter what stresses life threw at her, the shed was her safe place. With a book in her hand and a tea by her side, she needed nothing more.

On this particular morning, Catharine had gone upstairs, after the end of Quiz Time, to soak in the bath. If reading was Laura's escape, the same could be said for Catharine and her love of luxuriating in scented bubbles. Living together was a balance of spending time as mother and daughter without getting under each other's feet. They both needed some time to themselves and mornings like this were when that happened.

When her mother retreated to the bathroom, Laura sat down on the new sofa in the old shed and looked at the brown paper parcel. The name said *Laura Jacobs*, which felt like a half-truth. Jacobs was her husband's name. Perhaps it was time to leave it behind. She lived with her mother, she could take back her maiden name, give in to her new life.

Laura picked up the parcel and turned it over in her hands to access the rear, where a thick strip of clear tape ran along. Over the months since she had been part of the Book Swap group, Laura had received many such parcels as this. Sometimes the books came from people that she had, in turn, sent parcels to. Some were anonymous gift exchanges, random novels from kind strangers. Today's new arrival was one of the latter. She did not know what the book was going to be, and that made unwrapping it even more exciting.

Even though she had just finished reading a thriller, Laura devoured all kinds of books. Unless it was something she had already read, she knew she was going to love it. Even if it was a duplicate, she could swap it with somebody else and the cycle could continue.

Taking her time, Laura slid her fingernails beneath the edge of the tape and gently prised it from the paper. If she was careful, she could reuse it when she sent her next parcel.

As she lifted the wrapping, she caught sight of the back of the book, a sea-green colour with black lettering and a small photo of an author she didn't recognise. Even before she flipped it over, Laura had guessed that this was another thriller.

The cover confirmed her suspicions. It featured a red-haired woman with smeared lipstick and the bright yellow title, *The Trophy Wife.*

Laura let out a low 'ooh' sound as she studied the picture and turned the book back over to read the description on the rear.

Her eyes glided over the words, her mind already guessing the plot as she read. It looked as though it was going to be a good one.

"Thank you, stranger," Laura said to the empty little room. It was de rigueur to add a post in the Facebook group to send actual thanks to the sender, but that could wait until she had flicked through the first few pages.

She sipped her tea and felt the rush of starting a new novel. Laura took the book in her hands, feeling its comforting weight and smooth cover, and turned to the first page.

As usual, Laura quickly became engrossed in the thriller's plot. So engrossed that she didn't hear the crunching of footsteps on the gravel path that ran along the centre of the garden. So engrossed that she didn't hear the turning of the door handle. So engrossed that she didn't notice the door opening, and the tall figure step into the garden room.

"How's your book?" Catharine asked, almost causing Laura to fly out of her chair.

"Mum!" Laura thrashed her arms instinctively, and the book flew from her hands onto the floor.

"Sorry, love! Didn't mean to make you jump."

Catharine bumbled over to where Laura was sitting and bent to pick up the book.

"Oh, I've made you lose your page, too. I'm sorry."

"Stop apologising, it's fine!" She felt like she could just about have had a heart attack, but, sure, it was fine.

Laura extended her hands to receive the book from her mum. When Catharine passed it up to her, Laura frowned.

"What's this?" she asked.

"It came out of your book. I thought it was your bookmark," Catharine said.

The 'bookmark' was a scrap of paper that looked like it had been ripped from brown card. It curled ever so slightly, as though it had once been part of a cylindrical shape, and time and the weight of the book had tried to reshape it.

Laura pulled it closer to her. There were two faint, almost imperceptible words on it and as she read them, Laura couldn't help but gasp.

"What is it, Laura?" Her mother instinctively put her hand on Laura's arm.

Laura shook her head and looked down at her mother, displaying the scrawled note.

"I don't have my glasses," Catharine said. "What is it?"

"It says," Laura read, "'*Help Me*'."

A stunned silence chilled the room. The two women looked at the note and then at each other. Laura turned it over, inspecting it for any further inscription, but there was nothing. Then, she held the front and back covers of the book, raising it into the air, extended as though it were a bird about to take flight. Giving it a gentle shake, Laura tried to agitate the pages without damaging them. There was nothing. She took the book back into her hands, leafing through the pages as though it were a flick book, hoping to find something else, an additional clue or more information to go on. There was nothing.

Laura looked at her mum, and Catharine looked back. Neither of them seemed to know what to say.

Eventually, Catharine spoke, breaking her daughter's concentration. "Do you think you should call the police?"

Laura frowned.

"That might be a bit over the top. I mean, I don't know who wrote it or why it's in this book."

She was still turning the paper over in her hands, as though the motion would shake out further clues.

"Is there anything else in there?"

Laura shook her head. "Just the note."

Eventually, Catharine spoke quietly. "Do you know who it's from?"

"It was one of those where you get matched with someone at random. I've no idea. I think I could send them a message online, though." She paused. "I mean I should. I have to, don't I? What do you think I should say?"

Now it was Catharine's turn to consider her reply.

"Well," she said. "If she… I guess it's a she?… is asking a stranger for help on a scrap of card in a book, maybe it's not something she's able to talk about in a message. It might be best to be careful."

"You've watched too many of those Netflix mini-series," Laura said, and tried to smile. "But you're probably right. And most of the people in the group are women, so, yeah. You're probably right there, too."

Laura didn't reach for her phone, though. Instead, she held the note, reading and rereading the words. Just as she had tried to figure out the book from the back cover, she now tried to work out the meaning held within the note.

"I can't help anyone," she said, locking eyes with her mum, and trying to hold back tears. "Look at me."

She was a recently separated woman on long-term sick leave with depression, hardly in any position to be helping anyone. She wasn't sure that she was even helping herself most days. If the sender had been looking for a hero, Laura doubted that the note could have ended up in worse hands.

CHAPTER THREE

Catharine sat down next to her daughter, gently lowering herself onto the soft sofa, and placed her hand on Laura's knee. As per the request, she looked at Laura. She looked directly at her and she smiled.

"When I look at you, what do you think I see?" she asked.

"What?" Laura said. All her thoughts were buzzing around the note, and the fact that she didn't know what to do, and even if she did know, then she probably wouldn't be able to do anything, anyway. Her mum's question was a jolt to her system.

Catharine patted Laura's knee gently. "Forget about the note for a second." Of course, there was no chance of that. "I'm talking about you." She lifted her hand up and brushed a stray curl from her daughter's face, a motion she had repeated so many times over the past decades. "What do you think I see when I look at you?"

"A mess," Laura said, trying to smile. "Your daughter," she added. "Who is a mess."

Catharine shook her head. "You might be in a bit of a mess. Things have been so hard for you, but look at you. You're getting through it. You're finding things to keep you happy. Every day you get up and you face your new life. Just because your life may be a little bit …"

"Of a mess." Laura managed the smile this time.

"Different," Catharine corrected. "Just because your life is different now, it doesn't reflect on who you are as a person."

"I couldn't make it work, Mum. Jamie and I …we were perfect, and it fell apart. I couldn't fix it."

"I know, love. I'm sorry. I know how hard you tried. You both tried."

Laura could feel the tears welling, and she dabbed at her eyes with the corner of her sleeve.

"Here." Catharine pulled a tissue from her pocket and handed it over. She was always prepared for everything and anything. Laura wondered how on earth she did it. "You're still my Laura, though. You're still the same strong, smart, loving woman that you always were."

That was enough to tip Laura over into a full-on flood of tears. Catharine looped her other arm around Laura's back and pulled her in for a tight, warm embrace.

"That's it," she said. "It's okay. Let it out."

"This is what I mean," Laura breathed through her sobs. "I'm useless. I can't do anything. Not for anyone. Not even myself."

"Okay," Catharine said. "You're not useless, but look, at the very least, why don't you try to find out who sent this? Can you do that?"

Laura sniffed and wiped at her eyes, pulling out of the hug.

"I have to, don't I?" she asked. Her words came out sounding more confident than she felt, but she knew it was true. She had to help.

Laura opened her phone and clicked onto the social media app. Most of the groups she belonged to were reading communities: Book Swap, Psychological Thriller Lovers, Turning the Pages, and all manner of titles with book-related pubs. She was also in a couple of groups where she chatted with the school friends she hadn't seen for so many years she'd lost count, and one that was dedicated to a particular brand of luxury handbag that she adored but knew she would never own.

There was no need to type in the search bar. A quick scroll down her timeline and the Book Swap group messages popped up.

An enthusiastic review of a book that she had recently read caught Laura's eye and almost distracted her from the task at hand.

Instead, she clicked through to the group page and looked for the contact details for the group moderators. There was a list of names, and the one at the top was the one she recognised from her previous chats: Becky. It felt instantly comforting to see the name of someone that she thought she could reach out to.

"That's the one," Laura said to her mum, but mostly to herself.

She was focussed on the task at hand now, but Laura paused before she started to type.

"How much should I tell her?" she asked her mum.

Catharine shrugged. "I'm not sure. Play it by ear, I suppose. Why don't you ask her if you can get hold of whoever sent you the book and take it from there?"

Laura nodded and turned back to her phone.

Sorry to bother you. I'd like to get in touch with the person who sent me something in the book swap. Do you know who it was?

Resolutely, Laura pressed send and watched the message indicator show that the words had been delivered.

"I'll put the kettle on," Catharine said

The two of them were never the type to turn to alcohol in stressful situations, but sometimes a cup of tea and a couple of biscuits helped to calm the nerves.

Laura had never had any cause to contact the group admin before, but she had seen them in the discussion topics, and it was a friendly, positive group. Even without knowing Becky, to whom she had sent the message, she had faith that if she could help, she would.

For the time being, all Laura could do was wait for a reply. Catharine brought two mugs of hot tea into the garden room, and the pair of them sat, neither knowing what to say, waiting for a response.

As she sat there, in what had been her comforting space ever since her father had passed away, Laura's mind skipped through theories and explanations. There was no real point in speculating, but Laura was already afraid that she might never uncover the truth behind the words on the paper. More than that, she was fearful of what might happen if she found out who had sent the note, and why.

Laura hated cliffhangers and endings that weren't explained. She wanted the ends tied up neatly and all the storylines to come together for everyone involved. What she didn't want was to open the doorway to a whole mess of trouble, and she couldn't be sure that wasn't about to happen.

CHAPTER FOUR

The reply from Becky didn't arrive until later in the afternoon, when Laura and Catharine had taken themselves back into the house and back into their usual daytime routine. They had already been out for a walk around the park, with Laura pulling her phone out of her pocket every five minutes to see if there had been a response. Now, the television was on, and the women were trying their best to distract themselves from thoughts of the note by watching trashy quiz shows, and talking about anything but the most important issue.

A short sharp trill from Laura's mobile phone split their conversation. Before opening her phone, Laura and her mother exchanged a nervous look.

"Is it her?" Catharine said, in an almost whisper, even though there was no one else there to hear them.

Laura looked at the screen and nodded. She gulped and read the message from Becky.

Hi Laura. I can't give out other people's details without asking them. Is there a problem?

"What did she say?" Catharine scooted across to sit on the arm of Laura's chair, craning her neck to see the phone screen.

Laura didn't answer. Instead, she tapped out a message, trying to catch Becky while she was online and hopefully still able to respond. She couldn't bear to wait a few more hours to get in touch with the woman who was waiting for her help.

There was a note in the book that I got from my swapper

Laura paused for a moment, wondering if that was the right word to use, before deciding that it didn't matter and continuing to type.

and I need to get in touch with her. Would you be able to let me have her name, please?

She pressed send and looked at her mum.

television. She aimed at the screen and turned up the volume.

"Laura." Catharine raised her voice above the mounting din of Breaking Point, one of those generic late afternoon quiz shows they had slipped into the habit of watching every day.

"Kilimanjaro," Laura said flatly, choosing to answer the question from the screen rather than address her mother.

"K2," the garishly dressed contestant said.

"It is K2," the quizmaster confirmed. A happy ding rang out, and the contestant's prize money display increased by a hundred pounds.

"Oh, for…" Laura began to speak.

"Laura!" Catharine snapped. "Listen to me. You can't keep ignoring him. No matter what is going on right now, you need to start answering these messages. How do you think you're going to set about helping this woman from your swap group if you won't even sort out your own problems?" As soon as she had said the words, she snapped her hand up to her mouth, trying to push the words back inside, or perhaps trying to make sure that none further spilled out.

Laura looked at her mother in stunned silence. Since she had moved back home, Catharine had been unerringly and quietly supportive of her. She wasn't expecting this outburst.

"I'm sorry, but…" Catharine talked again.

"No. You're right. It's okay." Laura grabbed the remote control again and switched the television off. "You're right, and I'm sorry. I should be the one who's sorry, not you."

"I didn't mean to…" Catharine spoke, but seemed unable to find the words she wanted to say.

Laura could see tears forming in her mother's eyes, and she pushed herself up, out of her position of comfort, to instead go over to comfort her mum.

"Hey. Really, I'm sorry. You've done so much for me. Just being here for me has made such an enormous difference. I can't even begin to tell you. I don't know where I would be without you. Stuck with him, I suppose. Trying to find a way out of that mess still. But thanks to you, I had somewhere to go." Laura was talking quickly, but she was moving slowly, her arm around her mother, sitting beside her, reassuring and showing the affection that she was spilling out through her words. "I would have been completely lost without you. I mean, I am lost. I'm still so, so lost, but without you…"

It was Laura's turn to lose her words. Catharine rested her hand onto her daughter's and gave her a sad but warm smile. This was not how either of them could have foreseen their lives. Mother and daughter alone together, Jonathan gone and Jamie now seemingly part of the past rather than the future that Laura had expected and dreamed of.

"Tonight, I promise," Laura said. "I'll message him back tonight."

Catharine let her eyes wander over her daughter's face, as if searching for the truth.

"I mean it," Laura said. "After we hear from Becky. When I've sorted this out, I'll talk to him. Okay?"

"Promise?" Catharine said. "You know I only want what's best for you, love, and I think that ignoring him like this, well, it isn't doing you any good. Not in the long run."

Laura wiped a stray strand of hair away from her mum's face and nodded. "I know. And yes, I promise."

Laura was beginning to think that ignoring Jamie was the only way to move forward with her life, but there was no way she was going to be able to do that while her mum was insisting that she got in touch with him. Burying her head in the sand had got her this far, but her mum was going to make her pull her head out and face up to the future. As if she didn't have enough on her mind without the minor detail of having to sort her own life out.

CHAPTER FIVE

Even after four months of not being at work, Laura's body clock was still set on waking her up before eight every morning. She had tried to let herself have lie-ins, but somehow, she had never slept any later than what she thought of as her pre-break-up self.

It was as though there were two versions of her now: the one that had lived a seemingly happy life as a married woman with Jamie, and the one that now lived with her mother in the home where she had grown up. She couldn't reconcile the two lives – everything was so different. She used to have a husband, a job, hopes, dreams and happiness. Now, she had endless hours of daytime television, mugs of tea and no clue where her life was heading.

The break-up with Jamie had blindsided Laura. One day they had been planning a holiday to Tenerife, and the next he was telling her it was over.

"I can't go on," he had said.

"You can't go?" Laura replied, looking up from the computer screen, where she was about to click to complete the purchase of their flights. "We can change the date, but this is the best one, with school holidays and…"

He stopped her mid-sentence. "No," he said. "I can't go on. Not *I can't go*. I mean, yeah, I can't go. I can't go on holiday with you, but I can't do this anymore. I…"

Laura had sat at the computer table, looking at the screen, her fingers hovering over the keys. It was as though her body wouldn't let her move. If she stayed still, perhaps what was happening would just stop.

"What?" she said, quietly.

"Laura, look at me," Jamie said. He reached out for her hand and guided her around to look at him. Still, she couldn't make eye contact.

"We could go somewhere else. I could look at Greece, maybe. France? You always said you wanted to go to Italy. How about…" She was trying to turn back to the screen, to stall, to stop him from speaking, because she couldn't bear to hear the words.

"Laura," Jamie said again. And when she didn't look back at him, once more, more loudly, he said, "Laura!"

"What?" she snapped. "What, what, what? What do you want me to say? I don't understand."

"You know as well as I do," he said, which was a lie, or at least a misjudgement on Jamie's part. "Things are… well, they just aren't right between us. You've felt it too."

She hadn't, but in the moment, she lost all sense of being able to speak up, let her side be heard. Laura finally looked Jamie in the eyes and listened as he talked. She let him run through all the things he had been feeling, that he thought – no, he knew – that she had been feeling too.

"We're two people that live together," he said. "We're not a couple. This isn't a marriage."

If Laura hadn't been so stunned by the outpouring of words, she would have broken down in tears. Instead, she sat, looking up at him, dumbstruck. Within two days, instead of booking a holiday for the two of them, she was standing on her mum's doorstep with a couple of small suitcases and no idea how she had got there.

Now, she was lying in bed, in her childhood home, looking at her phone screen, and wondering what on earth she was getting herself into. Was this all the start of the adventure she needed to get her out of the house and start her recovery from her failed relationship? Or was she about to set off down a part that would lead to nothing but trouble?

There was no response from Becky that night, and Laura took it as an excuse not to reply to Jamie. She had promised to get in touch with him after she heard from Becky, after all.

The message from Becky finally through between the time that Laura went to bed that night and when she woke the following morning.

Becky had written:

> **I've talked to your gifter, and she's happy for me to give you her name. It's Carley Brooks. You should be**

able to find her by searching in the group.

Carley Brooks. It wasn't a name that Laura recognised, but then again, the group had over seven thousand members. It was unlikely that she would have recognised any but the most prolific posters. Some members loved sharing all of their book reviews, latest finds and lists of swaps, whilst others, like Laura, lurked in the background, enjoying the recommendations and the community vibe of the group. She had made comments on a few posts, and always took part in the exchanges, but her online life mirrored her real-life persona. She mostly kept herself to herself.

Until now.

Laura thought for a moment and then replied with,

Thanks Becky. I will.

Then, before setting about finding Carley's details from the group, Laura pulled herself out of bed, threw her dressing gown over her pyjamas, slipped her feet into her slippers and ran downstairs.

"I've got the name of the woman who sent the book," Laura shouted, as she made her way to find her mum.

The living room and kitchen were both empty. Catharine was in the garden, sitting at the small wooden picnic table with a mug of coffee.

"There's more in the pot," she gestured towards the door. "I thought you were still asleep."

"I was. I just woke up and saw the messages from Becky. Did you hear what I said? I know who sent the book," Laura said. "She must have heard from Carley late last night. Carley's the woman. The gifter. Sender. Whatever."

Catharine nodded. "I know what you mean. So, have you messaged her? This Carley?"

"No. I came straight down to you. I'm not sure what to say. I mean …how do I start?" Laura perched on the bench next to her mum.

"Sometimes," Catharine said, "The best thing to do is to not overthink it, and just do it. Open up your messages and start to type. See what happens."

Laura paused and raised her eyebrows. "Really?"

"Try it," Catharine said. "Can I get you some coffee?"

"Stay with me while I …" Laura began to say, but Catharine was already up on her feet and walking towards the kitchen.

"You can do this," she said, without looking back.

Laura watched her mother walk until she entered the house and then looked down at her phone. "I do not know what I am going to say to you, Carley," Laura muttered. "But I am going to work it out, and I am going to help you."

It was easy enough for Laura to find Carley's profile once she had the name. She searched the group members and clicked on the name *Carley Brooks* to bring up the profile.

Carley Brooks.

There were over seven thousand people in the group. Laura had never seen Carley's name mentioned before, or at least she couldn't remember seeing it, but suddenly it was the most important name in the world.

The profile didn't shed much light on Carley's life. There was a standard profile photograph, a smiling dark-haired woman wearing a bright pink t-shirt. A complete stranger to Laura. The *About Me* page didn't contain any information that Laura could see. The details were either absent or hidden from the public.

"Quite right, too," Laura mumbled to herself.

The posts on Carley's page showed only the sequence of profile photos that she had switched through over the years. As with her other details, the ins and outs of Carley's everyday life were invisible to the anonymous, unknown observer.

"Do you not want to share, or are you worried about who might see?" There was no one to hear Laura's question, but she had to ask.

Laura clicked on the *Message* button to connect to the page where she could, finally, contact Carley.

The empty text box sat waiting for Laura to compose a message, Carley's name and tiny profile picture at the top of the page. It looked like a blur of pink and brown, nothing more, but Laura focused on that picture, and tried to imagine the woman at the other end of the message. She had asked for help, and Laura was going to respond.

Sorry to contact you out of the blue. You sent me a book through the group.

Laura paused, wondering whether to add anything else. If Carley wasn't able to talk about whatever was happening over messaging, at least Laura wouldn't be putting her in a difficult situation, if she left the message open. But then, should she be clear from the outset that her aim was to give the help that Carley had asked for?

What was taking her mum so long with the coffee? Laura wondered. She lifted her head, trying to see inside, but she knew really that Catharine was giving her the space and time to work through this alone.

"I can help you," Laura said. "I can do this."

She carried on typing.

I got your message. Can you talk?

It seemed too much, too obvious. If someone was monitoring Carley's messages, if the help she needed was something she had to send a note in a book to seek out, perhaps this approach was too direct.

Laura deleted the last three words and changed them

I got your message. Can we talk?

Still not completely sure of herself, Laura lifted her eyes in thought and then, with conviction, pressed the send button.

"I hope I've said the right thing, Carley. And I hope you are okay."

CHAPTER SIX

As the message flew through cyberspace from Laura to wherever Carley was, she got up and made her way into the house to find the coffee that her mum had promised.

Catharine was already sitting in the living room, waiting for her, and Laura flopped down onto the sofa next to her mum.

"Are you okay?" Catharine asked.

Laura nodded. She was as *okay* as she could be, all things considered. Tense, and filled with anticipation, but *okay*.

Catharine took a sip of her coffee and put her mug down on the little table. When she turned to her daughter, Laura knew immediately that she had something serious to say. Her face was steady and emotionless; it looked as though she had been building herself up to speaking all the time that Laura had been outside in the garden.

"What is it?" Laura asked, anticipating what was to come.

"Darling, I know that all of this *note* business is taking up your energy at the moment, but do you remember that you promised you would talk to Jamie? After you had heard back from the Book Swap lady. Becky, was it?"

"Becky, yes," Laura said, answering the question rather than responding to the rest of the sentence.

"And you haven't talked to him yet, have you?"

"Apparently you know that I haven't," Laura said, in a sharp tone that she instantly regretted using.

"Well, yes, I do know," Catharine said, ignoring her daughter's misstep. "Because he messaged me."

Laura jumped back in surprise at this. Jamie and her parents had always been close, but his real connection had been with her father. She could imagine him exchanging countless text messages with her dad, and was sure that he probably had when Jonathan had been alive, but the thought of him sending a message to her mum seemed alien.

"Why?" was all she could manage to say.

"Well, love. I think because he has messaged you quite a few times, and you aren't replying to him. I know it was hard at first and you both needed that time and space, but …"

"But it's been four months and I should be over it by now?"

"I'm not saying that, Laura. Not at all. No one is expecting you to be friends. It's not about that. It's going to take as long as it takes." Catharine's gaze was so calm and loving that Laura's defensiveness began to subside.

"I'm sorry," she said. "It's just that every time I think about talking to him, or even replying to his messages, it reminds me of what I've lost. It reminds me that he isn't my husband anymore. Not really, anyway. You know, we always used to send each other silly messages, and now, I know there won't be any of that anymore. The only texts we will send each other and going to be about ending our marriage, getting divorced, and I don't think I can handle it."

Catharine listened and let Laura spill all of her feelings out. The couple had been married for five years and had been best friends for four more before that. She knew Laura hadn't only lost her husband, she had lost the man who had been her best friend. After Jonathan's death, Catharine understood only too clearly how that felt.

"It's understandable that you want to put it off, love," she said. "But once you start to talk to each other about what happens next, I think it's going to be good for you." Laura raised her eyebrows and opened her mouth to cut in, but Catharine raised her hand to stop her. "And I know it doesn't feel that way. I know, really I do, but right now you are stuck. You know that, don't you?"

Laura closed her mouth again and acknowledged that she did indeed know.

"The only way you can move forwards with your life is to deal with this situation. Talk to Jamie and make some plans."

"We had plans. We had plans for a future. We were booking a holiday. I was going to talk to him about starting a family. And instead …"

Laura felt her eyes fill with tears again. It was becoming a regular event.

"And none of it is fair, love. You deserve that happiness that you were looking forward to. You do." Catharine reached out and embraced her daughter again. "And in the future, there's no reason and every chance that you are going to find happiness. But my dear, beautiful Laura, that isn't going to be with Jamie. You know that, don't you?"

Laura had her face pressed hard against her mother, stopping herself from wailing out the anguished emotions she felt. It wasn't fair. Catharine was right. How had everything she had once thought was forever ended so suddenly and absolutely? There was no going back to the past, but moving on to the future seemed impossible when she didn't have any idea what that future would be built around.

"Yes," Laura breathed. A weak, reedy word that floated from her mouth and could hardly be heard. A truth that she didn't want to hear, let alone admit to.

She could just imagine, in that moment, speaking the same phrase that had been written on the note in the book. She needed help just as much as anyone else. Help to rebuild her world and move on with her life.

"Help me," she thought. *"Help me."*

As the words span around her mind, she clung on to her mother and let the tears flow.

CHAPTER SEVEN

When the reply from Carley arrived, it had no mention of the note. It didn't even seem to acknowledge the second part of the text that Laura had sent. Carley's message simply said,

Hi Laura. Was the book okay? I saw that you like thrillers, and I thought you'd enjoy the one I sent.

Laura read this, and then looked at the screen, trying to work out if there was some kind of hidden meaning behind the words. Was Carley trying to ask if she had found the note, and whether she could help her? Did '*was the book okay*' mean '*was the note okay*'? Did you get the note?

"Am I reading too much into this?" Laura mumbled. "Why is this so difficult? I can't just blurt it out, though. What if Carley is in danger?"

Laura looked down at her phone and typed again.

The book looks good, thanks. How are you? Is everything okay?

The reply came back almost instantly.

Fine, thanks. Hope you're well too. Let me know what you think of the book!

"She's trying to end the conversation," Laura said, trying to repress the panic in her voice. "But she says everything is fine. Should I just come out and mention the note? Is it time? I don't want her to think I'm some kind of …well, I don't know what."

Catharine looked into Laura's pleading eyes. "I wish I had all the answers," she said. "I don't know. I really don't. But yes, perhaps you're right. Maybe you should ask her. She says she is fine, so …" Catharine shrugged. "I'm sorry that I'm not being more helpful, love," she said.

"Oh Mum, it's not your fault," Laura smiled as much as she could manage under the circumstances.

Catharine shook her head. "I don't feel like I have been much use to you at all," she said. Laura could see the tears welling in her mother's eyes, even though Catharine was trying her best to hide them.

"That's not true," Laura said. "Hey. You have done everything you possibly could for me. You always have. You gave me somewhere to stay. You spend all your time with me, when I'm sure there are plenty of more interesting and important things that you could be doing."

Catharine cut in. "There's nothing more important than you. Before you came to stay, I hardly did anything anyway. I did what we do now, but alone. I've been so lonely since your dad …" Even after four years, it was still difficult for Catharine to say the word.

Laura nodded in understanding. "I know, Mum. And I'm sorry I didn't spend more time here with you before. I'm here now because I needed you …I need you …and I didn't see for all that time that you needed me. I'm so sorry."

Catharine tightened her lips and finally looked back at her daughter. "You had your own life to live. You still do. I need to look after myself and get on with my own life. Your dad would never have wanted me to be sad and lonely without him."

"We can't help it, though, can we?"

For a moment, the two women sat and let the truth hang in the air between them. Jonathan's death had left a space that nothing could fill, but it was something that mother and daughter barely spoke of.

"This note. I don't know what's going to happen, but I think you found it for a reason," Catharine said.

"I wish I knew what that was," Laura sighed. She looked back at her phone. "I'm trying to do the right thing, and say the right things, but, as usual, I have no clue what I'm doing."

Catharine shrugged. "Maybe it's time to just come out with it and ask her. Ask Carley if she wrote the note and if she needs help. You can only do something when you know what needs to be done."

Laura nodded, just once, and wrote her next message to the stranger from the Book Swap group.

I found something in the book. Did you send me a note?

It was still beating around the bush somewhat, but Laura still felt the need to protect Carley as much as she could. Just in case there was someone monitoring the messages at her recipient's end.

A note? No, sorry. I just wrapped it and put your address on the parcel.

Laura was about to speak to her mum when she saw the flashing dots on the screen that meant Carley was typing another message. She waited.

What did it say?

Laura flashed her eyes up to Catharine, without speaking, and typed a response.

It said, *'help me'*.

She pressed the send button before she had time to second guess herself, and Catharine nodded in encouragement.

"There," Laura said. "Let's see what happens now."

Catharine put her hand onto her daughter's and gripped it tightly.

Blooming heck.

came the response. Laura and Catharine exchanged another look, and Laura couldn't help but smile at the mild-languaged response. It was a phrase she often used herself. Then another message came through from Carley.

And that was in the book that I sent to you? Like someone had written it?

Laura replied immediately.

That's right. You don't know anything about it?

Carley's response was just as fast.

No. Nothing.

Then Laura waited for the rest of Carley's reply.

I have to admit something. I haven't actually even read the book. I'm trying to think where I got it from.

Laura stared at the text. It was confirmation that Carley really hadn't left the message. But if she hadn't, who had? It could have been anyone, at any time. The message might have sat there in the book, undiscovered for weeks, months or even years before Laura found it. When the note fell out of the book, Laura felt a sense of urgency, almost as though the note had been written right there and then and left for her to find. She never stopped to consider that it hadn't been written by the person who had sent the book to her. The text from Carley stopped her in her tracks.

"Are you okay?" Catharine asked. "What's wrong?"

"It wasn't Carley. She didn't write the note," Laura explained. Her voice was thin with tension.

Have you contacted the police?

Laura caught her breath and showed the phone screen to Catharine.

No. Not yet. I thought I would try to find out who the message was from first. I didn't have much to tell them. I still don't know what I could say to them.

I think you should get in touch with the police. Just in case.

Just in case of what? Laura wondered.

Okay.

Laura typed. Then the response from Carley came:

Then let me know what happens. Are you at home this evening?

"I'm at home every evening," Laura replied out loud. She didn't type that, though. Instead, she wrote:

Yes, why?

Carley's response was rapid.

Can I phone you? Later?

Laura let out a tiny squeak. "I'm no good on the phone, Mum. What am I going to say to her?"

"Well, if you're going to phone the police and tell them what you've found, you're going to have to make a call, anyway. It's good for you to get used to talking to people again."

"A stranger from the internet and the police? Not really what I imagined when I thought about expanding my social circle."

"Oh Laura," Catharine smiled. "Take it one step at a time."

Laura nodded and tapped out a message to Carley.

Sure. I'll get in touch with the police and talk to you later then.

If Carley wasn't going to be home until evening, Laura reasoned that she could put off making the phone call to the police until much later in the day. She would have to do it eventually, though. That was that. She had committed herself to at least the two phone calls. Beyond that, she had no idea what was going to happen

CHAPTER EIGHT

When Laura and Catharine had finished their dinner and shared the job of washing up, Catharine set about making tea for the pair of them.

"Go and get settled," she said, waving her daughter through to the living room.

"Do you think it's too late to phone the police now?" Laura said, making a show of looking at the time on her phone.

Catharine said nothing, but gave Laura a stern look.

Laura sighed. "I know, I know. It's only seven o'clock. I just… well, you know what I'm like," she said.

One of the best things about living with her mother was the familiarity that existed between them. Laura had moved out of her childhood home seven years ago, but had never gone more than a couple of days without spending time with her parents. Before her father had passed away, she and Jamie had eaten Sunday dinner with her parents every week without fail. Sometimes she would cook, sometimes Catharine, and sometimes the four of them would go out for dinner in a restaurant or end up in a country pub at the end of a walk through the woodland near their home.

Without Jonathan, something had changed. They started to skip the tradition, one week, then two, and before they knew it, their weekend meal together was just another memory. Laura still visited, but Jamie would increasingly stay at home.

She hated to admit to the thought, but Laura sometimes wondered whether he had only ever accompanied them to spend time with her father, talking about football and whatever feat of engineering her dad was tinkering away at in the shed that week.

Although he had never shared any signs of grief when her father passed away, she knew that Jonathan's death was a loss for Jamie, too.

Catharine knew her daughter inside out, and Laura had that same familiarity with her mother. The two of them were a tight-knit pair. Their closeness only grew as the distance between Laura and Jamie expanded.

"Come on, love. It's going to be fine," Catharine said, ushering Laura through to the sofa.

She was well aware that Laura had never been fond of speaking on the telephone, but she didn't know what a struggle it had been for Laura to take a job where speaking on the phone was one of the main parts of her role. Over the years that she had worked at the estate agency, Laura had created strategies to build her confidence in dealing with clients.

When Laura was dressed in her smart work suits, her hair ironed poker straight, and her standard mascara and lip-gloss combo were in place, she could play the role of Confident Laura.

Confident Laura was a part she had left behind in her old life with Jamie. Her suits were still in the wardrobe of her marital home, unnecessary to this, her new stay-at-home-and-mope persona. As she sat with the phone in her hand, Laura wished she could slip into her work clothes, that she had time to straighten her unruly hair, and pretend for just a few minutes that she was Confident Laura again. Instead, she was the Laura who sat around her mother's house in jeans and a T-shirt. There had been some days, in the beginning, that she hadn't even bothered to brush her hair, let alone take the time and effort to straighten it. She had got past that phase, at least.

When she had first moved back home, nothing seemed important. Attempting to look nice, or even to take care of herself, was the least of her worries. Four months on, although the change had come so gradually that Laura hadn't realised that it had happened, she was finding her 'new normal'.

Of course, part of that was down to Catharine's support. And again, as Laura looked at the phone, her mum was there for her.

"It'll be fine," she said again. "What's the worst that can happen?"

"Uh, they could arrest me for wasting police time?" Laura said, with a half-smile. Even saying the words began to thaw her anxiety.

Catharine shook her head and smiled back. "That's not going to happen. You're letting them know about something you've found. Even if they can't do anything right now, you're doing the right thing by telling them about it. You've done all you can so far."

Laura nodded in return. "Which isn't much," she said. "But, okay."

She tried to imagine herself dressed as Confident Laura, sat a little taller in her chair and lifted her head just a little higher. If she couldn't be Confident Laura right now, at least she could channel the person who she used to be.

Someone needed help, and she and Carley were the only people that knew.

Laura tapped out the number for the non-emergency police desk and waited as the phone rang out.

When the line connected, she was greeted by a gruff male voice.

"Police Officer Shawcross speaking. Can I take your name, please?"

"Uh, Laura. Laura Jacobs." The surname was an instant reminder of her break-up, and she frowned as she spoke the name.

"Miss, Mrs, Ms…" Shawcross asked. "Something else?"

"Mrs," Laura replied, and then wondered for a moment if she was a Miss or even a Ms now that she and Jamie were separated.

"And your address, Laura?"

"I'm living with my mum at the moment," Laura said, unsure whether the officer was going to check her records to make sure she was giving her registered address.

"I'm sorry, I don't know your mum's address," Shawcross sighed.

"Yes. Sorry." Laura reeled off the address, her face beetroot red. Channelling Confident Laura was not working at all. She was floundering and feeling out of her depth.

"How can I help you?"

Laura looked at Catharine again for more moral support and then spoke.

"I don't know if you can, really. I found something, a note. Er, I got a book through the post and there was a note inside it."

"A note?"

"Yes. It said, 'help me'. Nothing else."

"And who was the note from? Do you know the person?"

"Well, the book was from one of those exchanges online. I don't know the woman."

"How do you know it's a woman then?" the police officer asked.

"I got in touch with the group admin and asked them who sent me the book." Laura sighed. This was turning out to be just as awkward and complicated as she had feared. "The admin of the group contacted the lady, and then I talked to her."

"And is she alright? Does she need any assistance?"

"Er, yes. She's fine. And no, she doesn't need any assistance."

"So let me get this straight, for my records, you understand," the police officer said. "You received a book, with a note in it, from someone you didn't know. You've tracked them down and asked them if they do actually need help, and they have told you they don't."

"That's right," Laura said. "But maybe someone does. Whoever this lady got the book from, or…"

"And I suppose you know who that is, too?"

Laura could feel tears of frustration forming. She was hot and her pulse was thundering.

"No," she said, ready to give up.

The police officer feigned surprise. "Well, Ms… Jacobs. That's the first thing you've said that surprises me. I thought you were quite the detective. Look, I have to be honest with you. From what you have said, with no idea of who might need help, or what kind of help they need, if any, there's not a lot I can do for you at the moment. I'll make a note that you have called, and if anyone else contacts us with any further information that seems related to this, er, case, then I have your details. Okay?"

"Right. It's just…" Laura tried to respond, but before she could say anything else, the police officer cut in again.

"Thanks for taking the time to contact us. You have a good day now."

The phone line clicked to silence.

Laura stared at the phone, not able to bring her eyes up to meet her mother.

"That didn't sound promising," Catharine said. "Are you okay?"

Laura shook her head, looked up at Catharine, and immediately burst into tears. If she couldn't even get the police to listen to her, what good was she going to be to whoever needed her help?

Either she and Carley were going to have to figure this out alone, or she was going to have to give up on the whole stupid idea. She was not Confident Laura, she was Stupid Laura, Useless Laura, and whoever was counting on her for help was going to be terribly disappointed.

CHAPTER NINE

By the time Laura had finished her call to the police and given herself time to calm down, it was almost eight. Around this time, she was usually winding down and settling in for the night. Not that she got up to anything vaguely exciting on any given day, not usually anyway. Procrastinating about making the call to the police now meant taking herself out of her familiar rhythm and out of her comfort zone.

With no conscious thought, Laura had tucked her legs under herself on the sofa, making herself into a tight ball. It was like a sitting version of the fetal position.

"I'm sure that Carley is going to be a lot more friendly than the policeman," Catharine said. Her voice was soft, and Laura knew she was trying to be as reassuring as she could.

"I know, Mum," she said. "She seems really nice. Well, from what I know so far, which is pretty much nothing. I'll just tell her what the police said, and..." She let the sentence trail off. What else was there to say? She didn't have any leads or any more ideas about what she – or they – could do to find and help whoever had written the note. All she could do was to hope that Carley had remembered where she got the book from, or that she had some other plan.

Laura clicked her phone open and went through to the messenger app. There she tapped in the words:

Can you talk now? Shall I phone you?

She expected a message back from Carley, but instead, the phone rang almost immediately.

Laura looked at Catharine and her mum nodded back at her towards the handset.

"I'd say you'd better answer her," she smiled.

Catharine moved over to the sofa to sit next to Laura and rested one hand on her knee.

Laura took a breath and clicked the answer button.

"Hello," she said. It was always a good place to start.

"Laura? Hiya. It's Carley." It was an unnecessary introduction, seeing as the call had come through the messaging app heralding Carley's name, but it was friendly and somewhat familiar, even though Carley was a stranger to her.

Laura was pleased to hear that Carley had a very similar accent to her own. Not so close that they came from the same city, but Laura could tell that Carley must be at least from the same part of England as she was.

"Another Yorkshire accent," Laura said, not trying to conceal the smile in her voice.

"Aye," said Carley. "I'm in Leeds. Whereabouts do you live?"

"Sheffield," Laura replied. They were about an hour's drive apart. Suddenly, the world felt like a much smaller place.

"Been there plenty of times," Carley said. "Well, I've been to the shopping centre, anyway."

Laura laughed. "That's as close as you need to get," she said. She loved her hometown, but the large shopping centre on its outskirts was definitely one of her favourite places.

They had a connection, something to unite the pair of them. But that connection was not the one that they were there to discuss.

"So how did it go?" Carley asked, bringing them back to the point. "Did you phone the police?"

"Uh, yeah," Laura sighed.

"That doesn't sound very positive. What happened?"

"Well, they were about as helpful as I expected," Laura said. "I think I sort of knew that what I had to tell them wasn't really enough for them to do anything about. All I have is a note in a book from someone on the internet…"

"Hello!"

"That didn't write the note and doesn't know who did."

"Well, when you put it like that," Carley said with a little laugh. "But I do have something that might help. Maybe not, but…"

Laura sat upright so fast that her mother's hand jerked away from her.

"What? What is it?"

"I remembered where I got the book from. Don't get your hopes up just yet though," she said. It was too late though. As soon as Laura had heard the words, her heart had started to race. She tugged on her mum's sleeve and mouthed, '*she knows where the book was from*.'

Catharine nodded.

"I picked it up in a charity shop," Carley continued. "I'm not sure that helps much though, does it? It could have belonged to anyone."

It didn't help much. She was right. If Carley knew *who* she had got the book from, they could at least have started there, followed the trail to find the person who had written the note. They. Laura had already started to think about her and Carley as a pair, solving the mystery of the plea for help together. Carley hadn't said that she wanted to be involved in the search; Laura realised she had made the assumption blindly without asking her. Still, Carley had been the one to suggest the phone call. She had all but volunteered to take part in whatever the heck it was that they were doing.

"Okay," Laura said, her mind racing as fast as her heart. "Could you go into the charity shop, maybe? Ask them if they know who donated it? Do they even keep records of things like that?"

"Gosh, I've no idea," Carley said. "I don't know. I mean, they must know who donates things? But I can't go into the shop. I bought it when I was away a couple of months ago."

Away? Laura braced herself for the news that Carley had bought the book in some other country, that this was the end of her search. There was no way forward. And a couple of months was a long time when it came to someone asking for help. Laura had imagined that there was no time to waste, that she was jumping to action to save someone in the nick of time. Whoever had sent that note had needed help two months ago. Who knew what could have happened to them between then and now?

Perhaps it was already too late.

Laura was silent. There were too many thoughts tumbling through her head to even know what to say next.

"Are you still there?" Carley asked. Her friendly accent rang out soft and strong.

"Yeah," Laura said.

"I was on holiday in Cambridge," Carley said. "Just a few days away. It was really nice actually."

"Oh, right. Well. I've never been," Laura replied, still unsure of what to do or say next.

"I finished the book I was reading, and I picked that one up in one of the animal rescue charity shops. It looked good, but then I didn't have any more time to read for the rest of the holiday and I think I must have put it back on my shelf and forgot about it."

"Until the swap," Laura said.

"Yep," Carley replied. "I'm terrible for cracking spines and dog-earring the corners of the books I read, so this one looked like it was the best condition I could send you."

"Well, I haven't started to read it yet, but it's already turning out to be quite the thriller," Laura said, more cheerfully than she felt.

"I don't know what I would have done if I had found that note," Carley said. "I would probably have taken it to the police and then given up once they told me they couldn't – or wouldn't – do anything. I really admire the trouble you're going to so that you can find out who left it. I wish I had the confidence to do that."

Laura almost laughed. "Confidence?" she said in disbelief. "I'm far from confident. I would hate for you to get the wrong impression of me. I'm thirty years old and living with my mum. I split up with my husband, or at least he split up with me. I can't go to work because I can't bear for them to see what a total mess I am. But at least I've started dragging myself out of bed before lunchtime now, so that I can fit another three hours of crappy daytime television into my crappy life."

Catharine stared at Laura open-mouthed, and Laura gasped for breath. The other end of the line was silent.

For a moment, Laura thought that Carley had hung up, but the screen showed that their call was still connected.

"Oh, I'm so sorry," she said. "Are you still there? I didn't mean to… well, you know. I'm sorry."

"Sounds like you needed to get that out," Carley said, her voice calm and understanding.

"A little, yeah," Laura said, managing a tiny smile. "Actually, a lot. I really needed that." She let out a breath that she didn't realise that she had been holding, and her mum stroked her hair gently.

"I meant what I said, though," Carley continued. "I wouldn't have been able to do what you're doing."

"I'm not sure that I'm doing much at all," Laura said. "I'm not sure what to do next."

"Well, it's a bit late tonight, but I could phone the charity shop, see if they can tell me anything? I think that's all we've got left to try."

"Okay," Laura said. "I don't know if we are going to get anywhere, but I think we have to try."

"We," Carley said, with a smile in her voice. "I guess that means we're in this together now?"

"That's up to you," Laura said, with the same smile. "You got me into this, but if you want out, then don't feel you have to be part of it."

"Laura, I don't even know what *this* is, but someone asked for help, and I have the feeling that you and I are the only ones that can do anything about it."

"Carley, I think that too." Laura took a breath and paused before saying, "If you let me know where you got the book from, I'll phone them in the morning. Let's see what they say and take it from there."

By her side, Catharine smiled.

Even if Laura couldn't channel the confident version of herself, a complete stranger had seen something in her. The complete stranger was becoming less of a stranger, though. They were forming a team. They were in it together. Despite Carley's belief in her, Laura knew that if she was going to help whoever had sent the note, she had the feeling that she was going to need Carley to help her, too.

CHAPTER TEN

Finding the phone number for the charity shop was easy. Although there were several stores listed, there was only one animal rescue charity. The link for Red Paw Cambridge took Laura to the shop's website, and there, right at the top, was a link that said '*contact us*'. There was an email address and a phone number, and Laura highlighted the information she needed to make the call.

"At least one thing has been straightforward," she said. "I've got the number."

Catharine was in the kitchen, putting away the breakfast plates.

"That's good, love," she called through. "Are you calling them now?"

"Do you think they'll be open yet?" Laura asked, before scanning the web page for the trading hours. "Oh, it's okay. They opened at half nine. Yeah, I guess so then."

She sat for a moment, looking blankly at the webpage on her phone screen. This was yet another step down the path to who knew where. More than that, it was another stranger she had to talk to.

"I don't know why I volunteered to phone up anyway," Laura said. "Carley was the one who bought the book, and I'm sure she would have talked to them if I had asked her to."

"I'm sure she would." Catharine walked into the room and gave Laura a wry smile.

"What?" Laura asked, genuinely perplexed.

"Hmm, nothing," Catharine replied, the smile broadening. "Just that maybe you're gaining in confidence now. You seem to be taking the lead now that you have someone to follow you."

"It's not like that!" Laura was nigh on indignant. "If Carley is in this with me, we are partners in it. I don't even know what this is, apart from craziness. What am I even doing?"

"Make the call. One step at a time, remember? Let's just see what happens."

Laura took a series of long breaths. In through the nose, out through the mouth, and then in through the mouth and out through the nose in case she had got it the wrong way around.

"I'm fine, I'm fine," she said, as much to herself as to her mum.

Catharine merely nodded and sat beside her daughter, waiting for her to make the call.

Laura steeled herself and clicked on the number.

The ringing tone was so brief that Laura almost jumped when the plummy tones of the woman at the other end of the line sounded out.

"Red Paw. How can I help you?"

The woman used the name of the shop as though it were her own name. Even from those few words, Laura could build up an image of the person at the other end of the phone from the way she spoke. She sounded like a friendly senior citizen, although that could have been Laura's preconception of the kind of person who works in a charity shop. She probably baked biscuits and took them to work for the rest of the staff, and got on with her knitting during her lunch break. At that point, Laura knew she was wildly generalising and letting her mind wander from the task at hand.

"Focus," Laura told herself.

"I wonder if you could help me," Laura said. She was always careful, when talking on the phone, to tone down her broad Yorkshire accent. Not because she was worried about people forming their own misconceptions about her, but because she had found from time to time that her broad Sheffield accent made it difficult for people to understand what she was saying.

Seemingly, the Red Paw assistant was having no such trouble.

"I'll do my best, dear," came the reply.

Now the problem was going to be explaining the situation without making herself sound like she had lost the plot.

"I have a friend who bought a book from you, and we are trying to find out who might have donated it. Would you keep those kinds of records?"

"Oh, well, sometimes."

This was followed by a silence from the other end of the line, and for a moment, Laura thought the woman might have misunderstood the question.

Then she spoke again.

"If it was a Gift Aid donation, we would have their details. They get sent off, though. Confidentially, you know?"

"Gift Aid?" Laura asked. "Sent off?" She didn't want to sound stupid, but she thought it necessary to understand what she was being told.

"Gift Aid. You know."

Laura obviously didn't know, but the charity shop worker explained.

"If we get a donation in from a taxpayer, we can get a little extra back from the taxman. And like they say, every little helps." She said it with a flourish of laughter, even though Laura supposed she had used the line many times before.

"Right. But you don't keep those details? You send them off somewhere else?"

"That's right, love. To be honest with you though, I wouldn't be able to tell you even if I knew. There are all these privacy laws nowadays, you know. Most things come to us anonymously." The woman on the other end of the phone sounded apologetic, almost as though she yearned for the days when she could disclose everyone's personal details.

Laura looked at her mum and shook her head.

"Right. Of course," she said. "It's just…"

"I'm sorry," the charity shop worker said.

The handset felt hot against Laura's ear. She wasn't sure what else she could say. Perhaps there was nothing. Or perhaps she should mention the note.

"Okay," she said. "There was a book, you see…"

But she could hear the woman at the other end of the phone talking to someone in the shop.

"Yes, lovely, isn't it? Doesn't look as though anyone has worn it. Oh, yes."

Laura listened to the conversation, only able to barely pick up the customer's replies. The shop assistant seemed to have forgotten about her.

"Thank you anyway," Laura said.

"Oh. Yes, love. Goodbye." The phone line clicked and fell silent.

Laura turned to her mother with a shrug.

"What now?" she asked. "Should I have told her about the note?"

"It didn't sound as though she gave you the chance to say much at all," Catharine said. "She couldn't tell you anything?"

Laura threw her phone across the sofa, and it landed upright, with its back to her. Every path she went down seemed to lead to a dead end.

"Why couldn't they have left a phone number, or an address, or just some way of getting in touch with them? If they need help so badly, why make it so difficult for anyone to find them? I thought I was going to do some good for someone, to be useful for once, but no, I'm just the same old Laura: no good to anyone."

Before she knew it, tears were flooding down her cheeks, and her mum was wrapping her arms around her, pulling her in to her chest. Catharine's hand stroked her daughter's head, and she murmured, trying to calm her.

"You're doing your best, Laura. Remember that this isn't your job. No one is expecting *you* to solve this mystery. It might just be that you can't do anything to find this person, let alone help them."

Laura's words were punctuated by sobs. "I found Carley. I found where the book came from. I was getting somewhere. I'm so close, Mum. I really thought I could do this, but now… I don't know where to turn. What can I do? This person needs me." She pulled back to look her mum straight in the eye. "They *need* me, Mum."

Catharine relaxed her hold and looked back into Laura's eyes.

"You've been through so much," she said. "And you're still going through a lot. This note, all of this, I know you want to help, but, Laura, it's not your problem, and if trying to track this person down is upsetting you, then I'm not sure you should do it. I want what's best for you. I thought that this would take your mind off what's happening with Jamie for a while, but it's only making you frustrated and sad now."

"Are you saying I should give up?" Laura spluttered through her tears.

"Laura, just stop and think about why you're doing this."

"Because someone needs my help."

“Someone left a note in a book saying, ‘help me’. That doesn’t mean that they need *your* help. You’re not responsible for the wellbeing of a stranger. You’re responsible for *your own* wellbeing.”

Laura knew that her mother was only trying to make sure that she didn’t over-commit herself, or maybe get her hopes of helping up too high, but in her state of heightened emotions, Laura took the words as a challenge to her capability.

“Then who is going to help them?” she asked. “There might be nobody else that knows that this person needs help. They could be relying on whoever found that note, and even if they don’t need *my* help, if I’m the only one who knows they are in some kind of trouble then *I* have to do something.”

She cleared her throat and reached over to get a tissue from the box on the table. There always seemed to be tissues around since she moved back to her mum’s, but she didn’t use them as often as she used to. Not until the past couple of days, anyway. The sadness she had been feeling over the past four months had morphed into an angry frustration since finding the note. She wanted to be the kind of person who could help someone in need, rather than being the kind of person always in need of help. To do that, she was going to have to step up.

Laura wiped her eyes and reached over for her phone.

"What are you going to do?" Catharine asked.

Laura clicked open the screen and started to tap.

"I'm going to tell Carley what happened and between us, we can decide what to do next. I'm not giving up, Mum."

She knew, in that moment, that not giving up on helping the stranger meant she was not giving up on herself, either. She wasn't going to let herself think of the person she was as Useless Laura any longer. Even if she wasn't Confident Laura, she could still be the Laura who was trying to get her life together and do something positive. That was the least she could do.

CHAPTER ELEVEN

Laura thought about sending Carley a text message, but there was too much to say to go through the process of messaging back and forth. Instead, she clicked on the phone icon and hoped that Carley could talk. As the phone rang, she realised she knew next to nothing about her new friend. She didn't know whether she would be at work or looking after children. She didn't even know if Carley had a family at home. All they had done was talk about the note, apart from Laura's brief outburst about her sad, messed up life, of course.

Laura felt a rush of relief when Carley answered the call.

"Hi Laura, what's up?" she said in a light, cheerful tone.

"You're not busy, are you? I can call back if it's not a good time?" Laura was all apologies before she even knew whether she needed to be.

"No, no, it's fine," Carley said.

"I didn't know if you'd be working or whatever," Laura replied.

"Well, sort of," Carley told her. "I work for myself though, so it's not like my boss is going to tell me off. I can take a break for a chat with my new partner in crime. Or whatever the opposite of that is. Partner in solving mysteries? Doesn't have the same ring to it." Carley laughed, and the sound of it calmed Laura and brought a smile to her face. There was something about this woman that had a positive effect on her mood.

"Well, I have to say our detective work isn't getting us far at all at the moment," Laura said. She had felt defeated before making the call, but Carley's nature somehow made her feel that they would find a way forwards. "I talked to one of the women at the charity shop, and to be honest, she wasn't much help. She wouldn't, couldn't, give me any details, so we're not any further, I'm afraid."

"Did you tell her about the note?"

Laura sighed. She knew she ought to have mentioned it to the woman in the shop. It could have made all the difference. "I didn't," she said, apologetically. "I asked whether it was possible to get a donor's details, and she started talking about privacy and confidentiality. Before I could explain, she was nattering away to someone in the shop and hanging up the phone."

"Probably the dear that served me when I went in," Carley laughed. "She almost forgot to charge me for the book, now I think of it."

"So, what do we do?" Laura asked.

Carley made a thoughtful humming noise and then fell silent while considering her reply.

"I could phone back and explain about the note," Laura suggested.

"Could do," Carley said. "But if she's going to give you the spiel about confidentiality again, it might not get us anywhere."

"It sounds like you've got a better plan," Laura said. Even though Carley hadn't mentioned anything yet, Laura could sense something brewing in her voice. She sat upright in her seat, causing Catharine to give a sharp, curious look. Laura shrugged and waited to hear what Carley had to say.

"Maybe," Carley said. "What about if we go into the shop? We could talk to them, face to face, you know."

"Go to Cambridge? To the shop? You think that would make a difference? It's a long way to go. It's not as though it's around the corner."

"It's not *that* far," Carley said. "I don't mind driving. I'd really like to meet you, and even if we can't do anything, we will have tried our best. And something tells me you could do with a few days away."

"Where would we stay? What would we do? I can't just …"

The thought of picking up and going on a jaunt across the country with someone she had only started talking to that week made Laura's heart pound. It wasn't the sort of thing she did. Not just now that she was separated from Jamie, but not ever. That kind of spontaneity was so far out of her comfort zone that it seemed completely alien to her. She tried to hide the panic in her voice, but Carley picked up on it anyway.

"I stayed in one of those chain hotels when I went. It was cheap, but not in a bad way. At least if we're there, if we find out who wrote the note, we can visit them. Find out what's going on."

Everything had suddenly become a lot more real.

When the note was just a couple of words on a piece of paper that had fallen out of a book, it was a mystery. It was an abstract idea. A puzzle waiting to be solved. It was a distraction, something to keep Laura's mind off her disjointed, unsatisfactory reality. Actually setting off in person on a mission to solve the puzzle and find the person who had written the note was a completely different matter. Laura realised as Carley spoke that she had been fascinated with the *idea* of helping someone. Leaving her house, making the trip to Cambridge, felt like a mammoth undertaking.

"Laura?" Carley spoke. "Are you still there?"

"Yes." Laura's voice belied her hesitance.

"Are you okay?" Carley asked.

Laura looked at Catharine, hoping she wouldn't see the apprehension in her eyes. She didn't want her mum to be any more worried about her than she had been over the past few months. She couldn't believe that before this phone call she thought that this mystery was what she needed to get herself on track. It was just another excuse to hide away from reality, a fantasy in which she was a heroine rather than a hopeless case.

Laura shifted position slightly to look away from her mum and try to avoid her gaze.

"I'll leave you alone a minute," Catharine said in a hushed voice, got up from the sofa and left the room.

Laura gulped and wondered how to explain what she was feeling to Carley.

"Do you think we are taking this too far?" she asked. "I mean, is this …should we …oh, I don't know what I mean. It all felt like a big adventure until it started to become so *real*."

Carley's voice stayed calm and reassuring. There was no hint of nervousness when she spoke. "We can't just leave it," she said. "Whoever wrote the note wanted someone to find it. Imagine if it were you or me. Writing that note could be their only chance to get out of a terrible situation. And if we don't try, if we don't keep trying, we're letting them down."

The line was silent. Laura sat alone in the room, her phone pressed against her ear, warm against her skin. This was the point at which her future life could go one of two ways. She could tell Carley that they had done all they could, that they had tried to find the person's name and address, that she'd reported what she could to the police, and that now was the time to give up. Or she could agree with Carley, do everything she could to find out who needed her help – their help – and then do everything she could to help them.

Imagine if it were you or me.

Laura had felt so miserable and depressed over the preceding months, but never to the point of reaching out to a stranger like the person who had written the note. She knew that whoever had written it must have been in desperate need to have sent her two words out into the world for strangers to find.

Laura made her decision.

"You're right," she said. "We have to. We have to help. If this is the only way we can do that, then you're on. Let's do this."

If she could have reached out and hugged Carley right then she would have. Laura vowed to save that for when they met.

"Well, like I said, I work for myself, so I can go whenever you're ready," Carley said, not missing a beat.

"I…" Laura paused again. "I'm ready when you are," she said, trying to sound self-assured. Her doubts were still present, but her mind was made up. She didn't know what she was letting herself in for, but the die had been cast, and for her, there was no turning back.

CHAPTER TWELVE

By the time they had ended the call, Laura and Carley had made plans to set off for Cambridge the following day. Carley was going to book the hotel and pick Laura up on her way down the M1 motorway towards their destination.

Rather than excitedly racing to pack a bag and tell her mum that she was going on a road trip with her new friend, Laura curled her legs back beneath her and switched on the television. Her mind was racing with conflicting thoughts, but she had committed to her course of action and the only way to remain calm and in control was to not think about it further.

When twenty minutes passed without her mum coming back into the room, Laura began to wonder where she was. She clicked the volume on the remote control to turn it down and listened out for the sound of her mother. From upstairs, almost inaudible, she could hear Catharine's voice. At first, Laura thought her mum was talking to herself. It wasn't unusual for her to mumble away as she went about her routine, and neither of them thought anything of it. This, though, didn't sound like the kind of chatter Catharine made with herself. It was as though she were having an actual conversation with someone. Laura realised that her mum was on the phone. It was such an infrequent event that the idea hadn't entered her mind.

Laura tried to concentrate on what she was hearing, focussing all her attention on making out what was being said, but the living room door was closed, and all she could recognise was the muffled rise and fall of her mother's speech.

Instead of persisting, Laura settled back onto the sofa, turned the volume up to a normal level, and waited for Catharine to join her.

It was at least another ten minutes before Catharine came downstairs and sat in her armchair.

"Everything okay?" Laura asked. Her focus had switched from the anxious anticipation of her trip with Carley to curious inquisitiveness about her mother's phone call.

"Not really," Catharine said. "Jamie phoned me." Laura could hear the tension in her mother's voice. "He says you're still not answering his messages."

Laura couldn't keep eye contact with her mother and turned instead to the television. She kept her focus firmly on Antiques Hunt and tried to keep her thoughts away from her ex-husband. The red team had found a wooden unit that turned out to be a butter churn and it could end up making them a decent profit.

"Laura."

The auctioneer suggested a start price of forty pounds, which was already double what they had paid for it.

"Come on now," her mother said.

The bids came in hard and fast and…

Catharine reached across to the table, scooped up the remote control and hit the red off switch.

"That's enough," she said. "I'm not going to have a go at you. I know how hard this must be, but you have to talk to him. He shouldn't need to be messaging me. I'm not his wife."

"And I won't be his wife for much longer." Laura span to face her mother. "I don't want to talk to him. I have no idea what to say. I don't know how to talk to him anymore. Every time I see him, I die a little more inside. I can't bear it. I can't bear it."

"You promised me, didn't you? You promised that when you heard from that Becky, you would get in touch with Jamie and see what he has to say. That was two days ago."

All Laura could do was nod.

"Then do it for me. Do it because you made a promise. I only want what's best for you, Laura. You know that, don't you?"

"I've been distracted, with everything that's been happening," Laura lied. "I know I said I would, but all I can think about it the note and whoever wrote it." She flopped back into the chair. "It's not a bad thing. All I have done over the past few months is sit around feeling sorry for myself and moping over Jamie. At least I've had something to take my mind off my own stupid mess of a life over the past few days."

"I know," Catharine said. "But there's a difference between distraction and diversion. You need to talk to him. You have to try to find your way through your own situation. You have to help yourself before you help anybody else."

Again, Laura nodded. She knew that if she spoke, she wouldn't be able to stop herself from crying. The tears were already budding in her eyes, and any words she said would lead to the streams of emotion that she didn't want to let out.

"He wants to talk to you. He wouldn't say what it was about, but I'm sure you know more than I do. That's why you're not answering him, isn't it?"

It was too late. Laura opened her mouth and let out one deep, chest-heaving sob.

"If I talk to him," she said, her breath coming in hard, heavy gulps, "it's only going to make things worse."

Catharine shook her head slowly.

"Things are what they are," she said. "You need to talk to him to move forward. It's the next step. It's what needs to happen. I know you want to go back, that you want things to be like they were between you, but, love, that's not going to happen. Things can't go back. You can't go back. All you can do is go forwards, and the only way to do that is by talking to him."

Laura nodded again, this time trying to hold back the tears and stop the shuddering sobs from exploding from her.

"I know," she said, her voice almost too quiet to be heard. "I know."

Laura nodded slowly. "Okay," she said. "I'll phone him after…"

"No more delaying," Catharine said. "Why not do it now?"

There was no getting around it. Laura knew she couldn't put off the inevitable any longer; her mother wasn't going to let her.

"At least let me get a drink first, or…"

"I'll get you one." Catharine pressed gently against Laura's shoulder, settling her back into her seat. "You make the call."

"All right!" Laura half-laughed. If it wasn't for the swirling nausea that she felt at the thought of phoning her soon to be ex-husband, the situation would almost be amusing.

"Let me give you some space," Catharine said, and got up, leaving Laura sitting alone in the room with only one way forwards.

When they lived together, Laura and Jamie had hardly ever phoned each other. They used the same messenger app that she had used to contact Carley. Actual phone calls were for strangers or serious conversations. Maybe that's what talking to Jamie had become. They had only had a handful of conversations over the few months since they had been apart. She didn't know what he was doing, where he was, or even how he was. Whatever the answers to those questions were, she had already assumed that he was coping with their separation much better than she was.

The breakup had been his idea, after all. It was what he wanted, not her. He was getting exactly what he wanted, while she was left with nothing. Before she had even managed to call him up, Laura was already sitting with hot tears streaming down her face.

"Brilliant," she said, out loud but in a hushed voice, so that her mother wouldn't hear.

Out of all the phone calls she had made over the past few days, this was the most difficult by far. How could it be that someone who had once, not so long ago, been her everything, could now be a stranger to her? How could it be that she could once talk to this man about anything at any time, and now couldn't even bring herself to speak to him at all?

Laura cleared her throat, dabbed at her eyes with the corner of her sleeve, and sat up straight on the sofa.

"If you can't help anyone else, help yourself," she breathed, and then clicked the button to make the call.

As the phone rang out at Jamie's end, Laura thought to herself that she would be happy if he was busy and couldn't answer. That would mean building herself up again though, because, as her mum would no doubt remind her, this wasn't going to go away. Nothing would be resolved unless she talked to Jamie. She was lost in her thoughts when she heard his voice.

"Laura? Hello."

His voice sounded out of context and disembodied, coming as it did down a phone line, but it was him. Her husband.

The man she had thought she was going to spend her life with, and was now learning how to spend her life without.

"Hi," Laura said. Her voice sounded so small.

"You okay?" Jamie asked.

There were so many answers to that question, and most of them would lead to either a flood of tears or an argument. Instead, Laura chose her words carefully.

"Mum said you've been trying to get in touch with me," she said. He would know, of course, that she had ignored the calls he had made and texts that he had sent, but seeing as he wanted to talk, she wagered that he wouldn't want to start an argument either.

There was the faintest hint of a pause at Jamie's end before he spoke again. "There's no easy way of saying it. I've been to see a solicitor, Laura."

She felt breathless, as though someone had punched her in the stomach, and she sat in silence, waiting for him to say something else.

"You know I had to, right? That's, er, it's the next step. So, I went to see someone."

"A solicitor," Laura said, her voice almost so quiet that it was inaudible.

"Yes," Jamie said. "They asked me if you have anyone acting for you."

It was a statement, but he seemed to be waiting for a response, as though it were a question.

"No," Laura said. Her voice felt like it was coming from somewhere else, or from someone else. She had disconnected from it.

"Right. Well, do you think you could…" He paused, as though trying to find the right words. "I'm sorry, Laura. I know this is hard for you. It is for me too, no matter what you might think. But you're going to need to talk to someone. A solicitor."

"You're sorry?" Laura said from her dream-state. "It's hard for you, is it? You're the one who…" She looked through the kitchen and caught sight of her mum, sitting in the garden, her back to Laura. Taking a deep breath, she levelled her voice and said, "I know. I don't want a fight. That's the last thing I want."

"It is hard," Jamie said, his voice wavering slightly. "I didn't want this to happen to us, but you know that this is how it has to be. Don't you?"

She couldn't bring herself to agree, because doing that would be admitting that there was no hope. There was no hope, and a part of her knew it, but there was a chasm between the facts and the acceptance of the facts.

We could talk about it. We could try again. We could try to make it work. Get some help. See a counsellor. Try again. Try, try, try.

She didn't let herself say any of those things.

"I know that this is how it is," she said instead. "I'll see a solicitor, okay?"

"Thanks." This time, it was his turn to sound quiet.

"I'm going away for a few days," she said. "I'll make an appointment for when I get back. If you can wait that long?"

"That's fine, Laura," he said. "Are you going anywhere nice?"

If they had still been together, Laura would have told Jamie everything about what had happened, and about what was happening. Perhaps he would have come up with suggestions, ideas or insights that she, Catharine and Carley hadn't thought of between them.

There was a deep sense of loss attached to the fact that she couldn't share any of this with him. It struck her as bizarre that someone else's problems could have been something that would have bonded Jamie and her as a team. They would doubtless have come together to find the right way forward. Now all she had was a stranger, who was becoming a friend, and a husband who was becoming a stranger.

"Just a few days away," she said. "With a friend."

She didn't add the last few words to pique Jamie's inquisitive nature but realised as she spoke that he could easily misinterpret what she had said. For a split second, she thought about clarifying, but talking about Carley would only lead down a rabbit hole she wasn't prepared to tumble into with him.

She wasn't part of his life any longer, and he wasn't part of hers. Whatever happened from hereon, she was going to have to face it without Jamie.

CHAPTER THIRTEEN

Catharine gave her daughter a sad smile as Laura headed out to see her after ending the phone call.

"How do you feel?" she asked, gently.

"Pretty much how I expected to," Laura said with a deep sigh. "Every time I hear his voice, it's a reminder of everything I've lost."

"I'm sorry, love. And I hope you don't think I'm being too hard on you, making you call him back, but…"

Laura shook her head, stopping her mum mid-sentence.

"No," she said. "I should have just answered when he messaged me. I've built this little bubble around myself and I've been living inside it for four months now. I would say that I've been living inside it quite happily, but that's not true. Even though I've built these walls around myself and tried to shut out everything that's happening, I've been shut inside with my misery, too. It's like a greenhouse, really. My sadness grows really well in there…" Laura forced a smile.

"Bubble, walls, greenhouse, whatever it is, I know it's hard to talk to him. Well done, love."

Laura nodded. "Thanks. It does feel like an achievement, even though it's nothing really, is it? It's something that any normal person should just be able to do: facing up to the things that they want to avoid." Again, she sighed. "And now I have to find a solicitor."

"Not that I was listening in, but you said you were going away?" Catharine said. "What's that about? Did I miss something?"

The prickles of hesitation rose as Laura considered how to explain the road trip to her mum. She inhaled and spoke.

"I didn't have a chance to tell you before," Laura said, almost apologetically. "When I spoke to Carley, well, we sort of made a plan."

"Sort of?" Catharine asked. "A plan?"

Laura tilted her head. "We did… make a plan, yes." She tried to sound more assured as she continued. "We're going to go to Cambridge, where Carley got the book from, and try to find out who sent it."

"What on earth are you thinking of doing there? You're going to walk into that charity shop and demand that they give you the address? The woman on the phone was quite clear that she couldn't tell you who donated that book, Laura. I'm sorry, but this seems like a complete waste of time."

Laura's breath caught in her throat at the sound of her mother's abrupt tone.

"Mum! You could at least pretend to be positive. I'm getting out of the house and doing something. Isn't that what you wanted?"

"Not like this, no. Not at all. Laura, this is madness."

"I thought you were all for me helping this person. You've been going along with this the whole time."

"Because it was just an idea, Laura. It wasn't real, was it? You were never going to actually go out there and find them. Not really."

"You didn't believe in me? You don't believe I can do this?"

"It's not about my belief in you, Laura. It's just impossible, trying to find one person out of however many million strangers live in this country. However many thousands live in Cambridge even. Do you know how many people live there? Shall we look it up?"

Laura shook her head as her mum carried on talking.

"I bet it is thousands. Trying to find this person is going to be like trying to find the proverbial needle in the haystack. And if you do happen to find them, then what? What are you going to do with that needle other than prick your finger? This is not just silly, it's dangerous."

Even though tears were prickling Laura's eyes again, she blinked them back.

"I never expected this from you, Mum," she said. "I'm not going to get involved in anything dangerous. I promise. But I need to do this, not just for whoever wrote that note, but for myself. I have to feel like I am doing something…"

"Then do something else. Bake a cake. Knit a scarf. Write some poems, I don't know. Something safe. Something here at home."

Laura realised suddenly that it was concern that she saw in her mother's face, not doubt.

"I'm going to be okay, Mum. Honestly. I'm going to be fine. I'll be with Carley the whole time, and I know you're about to cut in and say that I hardly know her, and you're right, but please, she's really nice and I trust her, I do, so please, please trust her too. We will stick together, and I won't do anything crazy, okay? I'll stay safe."

Catharine let out a huge breath. It was as though a tense band had been removed.

"Oh, Laura, I'm just worried about you. I'm sorry. I couldn't imagine what I would do if anything happened to you. I've been so worried about you over the past few months. You've been so sad, and I've felt useless. I couldn't do anything to make you feel better. All I could do was give you a place to stay and try to keep you safe and take your mind off things. I've got used to our little routine here. I want you to be happy again, but more than that, I want you to be safe. I'm just… well… if whoever wrote that note is in danger, you could be in danger, too."

Laura did not know if the path she was taking was going to lead her somewhere dangerous. That much was true. Although she and Carley had touched on that idea, they had focussed more on the fact that there was someone in need of help, and that they were the only ones able to provide it.

"I promise," Laura said, her voice earnest. "I won't do anything that could get me into any kind of trouble. I love you, and I love that you care about me so much, I really do. But, Mum, I need to do this. I need to do it for whoever wrote the note, and I need to do it for myself."

Catharine bit her lip and looked at her daughter.

"You keep your phone with you all the time," she said. Her voice reminded Laura of the way she used to talk to her when she would go out in the evenings as a teenager. "If there's even the slightest hint of any kind of trouble – any kind at all – you phone the police, okay? You promise me, Laura."

"I promise, Mum. There won't be, but I promise, okay?"

The women sat facing each other, the air between them taught with emotion: the chill fear of loss and the warm comfort of love. Both knew the pain of losing someone, and though neither could imagine losing the other, Laura knew that the most important thing right now was to find not only the woman who had written the note, but to find herself.

CHAPTER FOURTEEN

There wasn't much time for packing, but Laura didn't have much to pack. Even if she had longer, Laura was used to travelling light. She was never one for taking anything unnecessary with her, and for this trip she was taking only what she needed.

She hadn't worn make-up since she was going to work every day, and even then, she would only apply the lightest layer of foundation and a slick of brown mascara over her lashes. Still, she pulled her make-up bag out of the drawer and placed it on the bed. There was something about applying an extra layer to herself that increased her confidence. It wasn't something she did to make herself feel more attractive, rather it felt like she was playing a different role when she was made up. She could be more than the person she was bare-skinned.

"*Better not let the feminists hear you say that,*" she smiled to herself.

Laura pulled her small suitcase from beneath the bed. When she had first moved back to her mum's house, this was all that she had brought with her. She thought it was going to be a short-term move, a few days apart, a chance for Jamie and her to get some thinking space. That was four months ago.

Since then, she had moved the rest of her clothes out of the grand, white-painted armoire that she and Jamie had picked up at an auction in Harrogate and paid more than the cost of the furniture to have transported back to their home. The armoire that still stood in the bedroom that she realised, more and more, that she may never enter again. The furniture and fittings that she had chosen with her husband stayed with him, but all of her personal possessions were now in the spare bedroom at her mum's house, and so was she.

When she came back home, or to where she now referred to as home, she would have to visit that solicitor. She couldn't bear to make a phone call to arrange it, but she stopped, mid-preparation to send an email and make an appointment. Putting it off wouldn't get her anywhere.

Maybe one day she would have custody of the wardrobe, but that was the least of her worries. She no longer cared about who got what or how much. If she couldn't have Jamie in her life any longer, what was the point in taking with her anything from her old home? Now she was surrounded by the fixtures and fittings that had been part of her life long before Jamie had. Her parents had solid, traditional furniture that had stood the test of time.

Laura sat on the brown velvet-topped stool in front of the large mirror on the dressing table and looked at herself. She was no longer the child or teenager that had lived in this room. She was no longer the person she was before she met Jamie, moved out, and married him. But who was she? Was she really the sort of person who travelled the length of the country with a stranger to answer a call for help from another stranger? Or was she the lost, lonely woman who couldn't even bring herself to go back to work because she didn't know who she was without her husband?

"What are you doing?" she asked her reflection in a soft, shaky voice.

"What are you doing?" her reflection said simultaneously, not breaking eye contact.

Laura shook her head and looked over her shoulder at the suitcase on the bed.

"Honestly," she said, "I do not know."

With Carley due to arrive any minute, Laura didn't have time to overthink her decisions.

She brushed her hair through and slung her brush into the suitcase. Then Laura added a wash bag with shampoo, conditioner and shower gel.

"You never know what you'll get in hotels these days," she told herself.

It was the first trip away she had taken by herself since she'd been on a French exchange visit with school. She had never had to travel for work, and she had always had Jamie by her side when she went anywhere over the past few years. Although it was hardly going to be a holiday, she wanted to be sure that she had packed everything she needed.

Phone. Charger. Book. Book for Carley. Another book for Carley. Kindle?

No, leave the Kindle behind. Or maybe she should take it after all.

She cast her eyes over the contents of the case, then pulled the zip around to fasten it before she could change her mind and add anything else.

When she got downstairs, Laura saw that her mum was standing by the side of the window, peering through the gap between the wall and the edge of the curtain.

"Do you know how crazy that looks?" Laura asked, with a little laugh.

Catharine batted her hand towards Laura without speaking, just uttering a shushing sound.

"No one can hear me!" Laura rested her case against the wall and sat down on the sofa.

"I know," Catharine said in a loud whisper. "I'm trying to be covert."

Laura laughed properly this time.

"You've definitely read too many of those Jack Reacher books."

"Reacher isn't a spy," Catharine said, in her regular voice, stepping back from the window. "You can borrow any of the books if you…"

Laura was already waving the idea away.

"Not for me, Mum," she smiled. "But thanks. You know what I mean, though."

"Have you got everything ready?" Catharine asked.

"I think so," Laura said. "Unless you can think of anything I might have missed?"

"Well, if there is anything, you'd better be quick, because she's here."

"What?" Laura almost yelped. She ran over to join her mum at the window and edged her out of the way so that she could peep through the curtain in her place. "Is that her?" she asked.

A dark-haired woman stepped out of the car and looked directly at their house. Laura ducked out of the way quickly so as not to be seen.

"I thought I was ready, but I'm not. I can't. Oh my... what am I doing? What can we do to help anyone?" Laura thought, but didn't say.

Laura stepped away from the curtain, and Catharine took her place again.

"Nice car, she's got," Catharine said. "One of those little red ones that you like."

"Oh," she acknowledged, barely able to focus on what she was doing, let alone to think about her new friend's car. "Nice." She gave her mum a smile and hoped that she didn't look as nervous as she felt. "Do I look okay?" she asked.

"Don't worry about that," Catharine smiled. Just as she spoke, the doorbell rang. "Now go and answer the door and see if your new friend wants to come in for a cuppa before you set off."

Laura was frozen to the spot in the middle of the room. Without even being aware of it, she was twisting the ring on her left hand, turning it in circles. She should have taken it off before now, surely. Why was she still pretending to be someone that she wasn't? It was a strange thought to have as she was about to meet Carley and set off on their journey together, but her thoughts seemed completely focussed on her ring, and why she had left it on despite everything that had happened.

"The door," Catharine reminded Laura, as Carley knocked again.

Laura snapped back to attention, brushed her T-shirt down and hurried towards the door. She tried to shake the obtrusive thoughts out of her mind. There was enough to be thinking about without worrying about what was going to happen when she returned.

Before she pulled open the door, Laura stood for a couple of seconds on the welcome mat where her mum always insisted she wipe her feet before venturing into the house. The beaming sunshine print smiled up at her, but did nothing to boost her confidence. Laura reached her hand out to the lock and twisted it to open the door.

There, in front of her, at last, was Carley.

CHAPTER FIFTEEN

The woman on the doorstep was barely recognisable from the miniature image that Laura had seen on the social media profile. Not that the image wasn't an accurate reflection of the real person, but that it had been so small and difficult to see that Laura hadn't been able to completely get a fixed idea of what her new friend looked like. Carley was a couple of inches shorter than her own fairly average height and had the kind of figure that Laura used to have before she stopped working out three times a week and started moping around her mum's house instead.

Carley smiled broadly and held out her arms for a hug.

"Hiya," she said, in the broad accent that was unmistakably from Leeds.

"Hi," Laura breathed in a mousey squeak that gave away her nervousness. She leaned forwards towards Carley and stepped out of the house to join the welcoming embrace.

"You alright?" Carley asked. "You're shaking."

"I'm sorry," Laura said, feeling her cheeks redden. "I don't usually, I mean I'm not sure, I…"

Carley hugged a little tighter. "Hey, it's okay," she said.

Laura cleared her throat, gave Carley a squeeze, and stepped back.

"I just spent ten minutes while I was getting ready, talking to myself asking what the heck I'm doing," she said, with a smile.

"I've been asking myself the same thing in the car on the way here," Carley said. "But we know really, don't we?"

Though there was still doubt in her mind, Laura didn't say anything, instead agreeing with Carley.

Then Laura looked over Carley's shoulder towards the little red car that her mother had mentioned. It was indeed the one that she wanted, if she was ever going to drive again. She and Jamie had been a one car family, and as he used the car for work and she didn't even go to work anymore, it seemed only fair that he was the one to keep the vehicle. Their car had been an old blue banger, nothing nearly as smart as Carley's car. She must be doing alright for herself, whatever she did. Laura realised she knew hardly anything about the woman that was standing in front of her. She worked for herself, but what exactly was it she did? No doubt there would be plenty of time to talk about that on their journey south.

"Something wrong?" Carley asked again, snapping Laura back into the moment.

"Just admiring your car," Laura said. "I'd love one of those."

"Thanks," Carley said. "I've not had it long. This is its first big drive out." Then, as if sensing a trace of apprehension, she added, "It's been absolutely fine all the way here, though. You don't have to worry."

Laura smiled. "I'm worried about a few things, but your car isn't one of them."

Carley nodded and smiled back. "Well, it's nice to meet you at last anyway, Laura. I feel like we've been talking for weeks."

It had only been two days since Carley's first reply to Laura; things had moved quickly. Now Laura realised she was moving very slowly.

"I'm so sorry. Come in, come in." She stepped aside so that Carley could enter the house, and even though she didn't ask her to, Carley wiped her feet on the mat on the way in.

"My mum is just through here," Laura said, taking the lead as they walked through into the living room.

Catharine was standing poised already, waiting to step forwards and meet their visitor.

"Mum, this is Carley," Laura said as they entered the room. "Carley, this is my mum, Catharine."

"Pleased to meet you, love," Catharine said, shaking Carley's outstretched hand with awkward formality. "How was your drive down here?"

"Oh, fine, thanks," Carley said. "I was telling Laura that I've been down to the shopping centre a few times. I know the road down here pretty well."

The three women smiled; the atmosphere was, on the surface, light and relaxed. However, there was an underlying sense of tension at the forthcoming trip that was planned.

"Can I make you a brew before you set off, or are you planning on getting going?"

Carley flicked her eyes over Laura's shoulder to look at the clock on the wall.

"I don't mind. What do you want to do, Laura?"

"Shall we get going? Unless you need a drink?"

Carley shrugged. "I'm easy, really. Thanks though."

"To be honest, I'm just itching to get on our way. The more I sit here, the more anxious I get, so maybe we could just set off?" Laura said it as a question rather than a statement, not wanting to make all the decisions this early on.

Carley nodded. "It was nice to meet you, Catharine," she said. "I'll have that brew when I bring Laura back."

"I might even make cake," Catharine said. "It'll take my mind off… well…" She stopped and looked at Laura. "Just be careful, the two of you, okay?"

"Of course," Carley said.

It was too late for Laura to question herself further. She looked at her mum, and her mum looked back.

"You have your phone. If you need me, or if you need anything, you call me, okay?"

Laura nodded.

"And don't get into any situations that you can't get out of. Don't do anything dangerous. At the first whiff of danger, you stop, and you call the police, okay?"

Laura nodded again.

"The very first whiff. Even if you aren't sure, you step back and you call the police."

"I know, Mum. I will."

The reality of what she and Carley were planning to do hit Laura like a slap. She had thought about it before, but perhaps never admitted it to herself until this point. Their journey could turn into something dangerous. They could be stepping forward onto a path that might lead one, the other or both of them into a situation that they hadn't planned for.

CHAPTER SIXTEEN

The journey from Sheffield to Cambridge was a solid two-hour drive. Once they had pulled out of the suburbs of the city onto the M1 motorway, it was the grey of tarmac and green of embankment all the way down to the only slightly less boring stretch of the A14 that led to their destination.

Of course, Laura barely noticed the lack of scenery or the proliferation of traffic. She and Carley started chatting the moment they set off from outside Laura's home and were still deep in laughter-filled conversation when they arrived at the hotel. Laura wasn't usually good with strangers, but talking to Carley was easy.

Carley pulled into the car park at the front of their hotel and switched off the engine. For a moment, the two women looked at each other, before Carley said, "Well, we're here."

The hotel was a square red brick building, with the chain's chirpy logo emblazoned on a board over the front entrance. It was clear which way they had to go, but neither of them was moving.

"Having doubts?" Laura asked.

Carley smiled. "Nope. The time for doubts was when the police told us they couldn't do anything, and we decided we were going to do the investigative work ourselves."

She sounded so confident. Laura could either be submerged by this or carried along in Carley's wave.

She decided on the latter.

"Come on then," Laura laughed. "Let's unpack and get a brew. I'm gasping."

It was just after three in the afternoon. Laura would usually have been about to settle down after her daily walk, and now, here she was in another city, about to spend the night in a strange place with a woman that was seeming more like a friend and less like a stranger.

They bundled their luggage out of the car and made their way into reception.

The hotel room was basic, but Laura's body still tingled with a mixture of anticipation and excitement. This was something different, something new, and possibly, as she reminded herself, something dangerous.

"I'd better let my mum know I'm here," she said.

Carley nodded but made no move to message any of her friends or relatives in return.

"I live on my own," Carley said, noting Laura's pause. "No one is going to be worried about me."

The comment left Laura with a tinge of unease. Should people be worrying about them? And what would it be like to not have anyone that cared where you were or what was happening to you? She might not have a lot, Laura thought, but she had that.

"Well, we can worry about each other," Laura smiled. "Or, hopefully, not have to worry too much."

"Yes," Carley laughed. "Let's go with that one." She picked up the tiny travel kettle and walked to the tap. "Go on, let Catharine know that we're here and I'll get the tea on."

"Thanks," Laura said, and wrote the message out to her mum.

Arrived safely. Miss you already. Everything is okay here.

She had the feeling that if she were to phone her mum instead, Catharine would end up becoming even more worried, and they would both be in tears. The downside to having someone to worry about you was the fear of that worry causing them distress. Although Catharine had agreed to Laura's trip with Carley and all it entailed, Laura knew it was with a heavy heart.

Her phone beeped with a return message almost immediately.

Call me straight away if you need me. Good luck.

"She says, '*good luck*'," Laura relayed the message to Carley.

"Luck would definitely be a good thing," Carley said. "Do you need to message anyone else?"

All along their journey down the motorway, the two of them had talked about books, social media, television series they had both enjoyed and the kind of trivial topics that strangers getting to know each other consider safe surface topics for conversation. Neither had touched on their personal situations nor private lives.

"I doubt my husband would care where I am, seeing as we've been separated for four months now," Laura said with a mock sigh. She tried to make light of the information, but saying the words out loud to her new friend was harder than she had expected.

Previously, when she had met anyone new, she had talked animatedly about her husband, how wonderful he was, and how happy they were together. Now she had a new narrative.

"Oh man," Carley said. "I think that's a conversation we can have over a glass of wine rather than a cup of tea."

Laura's stress melted and she let out a hooting laugh. "How about a whole bottle?" she suggested with a grin.

Talking about Jamie and still having the ability to smile was a new feeling for her, and it was one that she could definitely get used to. Carley had never known her as *Laura, Jamie's wife*, or even *Laura, Jamie's girlfriend*. All Carley knew her as was *Laura*. She could be herself here, and it was a liberating feeling.

CHAPTER SEVENTEEN

Once they had settled into the hotel and had dinner, the conversation turned to more personal matters. They were getting to know each other well enough to start asking more intimate questions, and for Carley, there was one main thing she wanted to know.

"So, you and your husband. You said that you've been split up for a while. What happened?"

Laura looked away, and fiddled with the end of her sleeve, distractedly.

"You don't have to say. I'm sorry. I shouldn't have asked." Carley said.

Laura shook her head. "No, don't be sorry. Really. It's just all so fresh, you know. I haven't spoken to anyone about it before."

If Carley was surprised, she hid it well.

"That's okay," she said. "I can't imagine how difficult it must be."

"The thing is, it's all very boring. Neither of us did anything wrong. Not really. He wasn't abusive. He didn't cheat." She took a deep gulp of her wine. "And neither did I."

"I didn't think you would have."

"You never know, though, do you? I mean, I know we are here, now, in this together, but we don't really know each other, do we? Not properly. For all you know, I could be the worst person in the world. I must have done something to make my husband walk out on me, right?"

Carley shook her head. "Sometimes nobody does anything wrong, and relationships just don't work out. Marriages don't work out."

"I don't know. I'm not sure that it wasn't meant to be. I still think that we could…" She stopped herself mid-sentence. Who was she trying to fool? These lines that she parroted out might work with her colleagues at work, or her neighbours, but what was the point in trying to pretend to Carley?

"We just didn't work as a couple. He was my best friend. Long before we were a couple. We were amazing together. Just not as husband and wife. As much as I would love to think that we could work it out some day, in all honestly, we can't. We won't. It's just not meant to be."

Laura could feel the tears welling, so again she looked away. As she dabbed at her eyes with the corner of her sleeve, Carley comforted her.

"When you think about it, splitting up might have been for the best… people stay together for years in unhappy marriages because neither of them has the balls to end it. They don't even have the courage to say anything. Instead, they plod along, wasting their lives with someone that they don't even want to be in the same room with. If it wasn't meant to be, then perhaps it's better that it's over."

Laura could feel her lips quivering, the emotion that had built up over her months away from Jamie shuddering through her body. She brought the glass back up to her mouth and took a deep gulp of the cold, dry wine.

"And perhaps it's time I accepted that," she said after swallowing.

This time, Carley didn't reply. She looked at Laura with such warmth and friendliness in her expression that Laura could hardly believe that the two of them had only known each other a few days.

"It might sound ridiculous to say this, under the circumstances, but I think I needed this."

"A distraction from your normal life," Carley said, a statement, rather than a question. "I know what you mean. Whatever happens tomorrow, I think something good has come of this."

"If you had asked me a week ago, I wouldn't have believed I'd have the confidence to drive down the country with a total stranger. No offence."

"None taken." Carley smiled

"I barely left the house. But this. Well, I couldn't just do nothing, you know. And I mean, we tried our best, didn't we? To find out what was happening."

"And now we are here. I don't know what we are going to find tomorrow, but we can deal with it."

"Do you have a plan?" Laura asked.

"Me?" Carley laughed. "Not really. Same as yours, I suppose."

"See what happens," they both said in unison.

Sharing the same bedroom with someone else for the first time in months was a strange feeling for Laura. Whether it was down to the unfamiliar room, the proximity of someone that she didn't know very well, or the thought of what they might come up against the following day, Laura found sleep hard to come by. Although the room had heavy blackout curtains, there was a chink of light that shone out above them, and Laura found herself distracted by it. She turned away from that side of the room, but then she saw Carley's sleeping figure and wanted to roll over again.

Her mind flitted from thoughts of what she was going to do or say when she visited the charity shop in the morning to what they were doing there at all, and then, when she had worried enough about that, she started to think about Jamie, solicitors and her entire uncertain future. There was nothing positive to focus on, and sleep seemed like an impossible undertaking.

In the other, identical bed, Carley seemed to have had no difficulty in getting to sleep, as Laura could make out the slight rise and fall of her sleeping breaths and hear the low snoring that accompanied them.

How nice it must be to be so contented and at peace with oneself that she could fall asleep anywhere, under any conditions. Carley seemed so self-assured and confident, whereas Laura was filled with anxiety and apprehension about what the coming day would bring.

At home, if she couldn't sleep, Laura sometimes opened up her Kindle and read until her eyes became heavy and the words no longer made sense. She had tried listening to audiobooks for a while but found that she would wake up with the book having finished, and having no idea where she had been up to at the point where she had fallen asleep. Maybe that would have been just what she needed tonight, though. She didn't want to click open her Kindle for fear that the light would cause Carley to wake up, so instead, she closed her eyes and tried to bat away all the thoughts that kept trying to infiltrate her mind.

Instead of worrying about what was to come, she let her imagination turn to the person who had written the note, trying to picture exactly who it might be or what help they might need. She wanted to think about why she was there positively, but every thought she had seemed to lead to another worry or concern.

"Focus on the outcome. Think about why you're doing this," she thought.

She had made the journey with Carley because it was the right thing to do. If she could keep that at the forefront of her mind, perhaps she would find sleep, and perhaps she could tackle whatever the next day threw at her.

CHAPTER EIGHTEEN

Even with the bare minimum of sleep, the women woke early. Laura didn't spend long getting ready, and she was pleased to see that Carley didn't either. They were both dressed for the day in jeans and sweatshirts. Carley tied her dark hair up into a messy bun, and Laura brushed hers through and let it fall loose onto her shoulders. She almost forgot that she had brought her make-up until she was placing her hairbrush back into her case. Although she doubted it would make much difference to how she felt, she smeared a thin layer of foundation over her pale skin, and applied mascara and lip-gloss. Sometimes it felt like camouflage, but today it was more like war paint.

Their plan was to take advantage of the hotel's buffet breakfast, and then head directly to the charity shop. After that, as both of them had said, they would see what happened.

They were out of the hotel before ten and on their way to the shop. Despite having visited the shop a few months previously, Carley had to admit that she needed help finding it, and put the address into Google Maps.

It was a short drive from their hotel into town. Carley parked up on a side street, and they climbed out of her little car.

"Maps says it's along here somewhere," Laura said. She tried to sound confident and as though she knew where they were going, but all she was really doing was following the directions on her phone. Following directions was easy; she wished there was some kind of guidance that would tell her what to do when she got to the shop too.

"You'd think I'd remember how to get there," Carley laughed. "I have a terrible sense of direction, though."

As they rounded the corner onto the main stretch, Carley grabbed Laura's arm and pointed up the road.

"There it is!" she said. "I remember it now." She slapped her other hand towards herself in a facepalm gesture.

Laura could just about make out a sign jutting out from the side of the shop with a large red symbol on it.

"Red Paw," Carley pointed. "Do you see it?"

The image became clearer as they walked towards the shop. It was indeed a large red paw, with 'Red Paw Animal Rescue' written in small letters along the bottom of the sign.

It only took a few more minutes for the women to find themselves outside the shop. In the window was the usual display that Laura was accustomed to seeing in charity shops: mannequins bedecked in colour co-ordinated clothing, old crates stacked to display floral crockery and photo frames, a typewriter with a sheet of paper placed as though ready for the writer to start tapping at the keys. Everything was normal, ordinary and unremarkable, but Laura knew that this visit to the charity shop was going to be unlike any she had experienced before.

"What if they won't tell us anything?" Laura said. "What if we've wasted our time coming?"

"We haven't come all this way for nothing," Carley said, her voice resolute. "We're going to stay until we find out how to get in touch with whoever needs our help. One way or another."

Our help. They truly had become a team.

Laura peered past the window display and on into the shop.

"And we haven't come to hang about outside either," Carley said, not unkindly. "Now or never, okay?"

Although part of Laura could easily have said 'never', and have turned back right then, they had come too far for her to surrender to the uncertain side of herself.

Carley stepped forwards towards the door, and Laura fell into line behind her as the two of them entered the shop.

Although Laura would usually have been easily distracted by the rails of clothes and especially the three floor-to-ceiling bookcases that stood along the far wall, on this occasion the two women headed directly to the till. The assistant standing at the counter was far from the elderly lady that Laura had pictured when she made the phone call only a few days previously Rather, she was a smartly dressed lady, no more than four or five years older than the pair of them.

The shop would have a pool of volunteer workers, of course, but seeing someone other than the person who she expected to encounter threw Laura even further off balance.

"Er, hello," she said, far more nervously than she had planned.

The woman looked the two of them up and down, clearly noting that neither of them appeared to be holding anything that they wanted to purchase.

"Can I help you?" she asked. Her tone was a peculiar mix of friendliness and caution.

Carley glanced at Laura and stepped forward to speak.

"I came in a few weeks ago, and bought a book from you," she began. "And I need to find out who donated it."

The shop assistant's expression appeared more interested as Carley spoke.

"Was there something wrong with it?" she asked. "If there's a problem, I can try to help you with that."

"Not exactly," Laura said, cutting in. "I think whoever donated it to you might be in trouble. We need to get in touch with them."

"Trouble? What kind of trouble?"

Laura took a breath and wondered how many times she was going to have to explain about the book swap, the note, and their mission to help a complete stranger. She gave the shop assistant a condensed version of everything that had happened so far.

"Basically, I just need your help," Laura said.

"We went to the police, of course." Carley thought it important to add the part that Laura had forgotten to mention.

"Of course," the woman repeated.

"But I'm afraid they weren't much help," Laura said.

"No help at all," Carley chipped in.

Laura shook her head. "Because they didn't have any information about who had written the note, or what kind of help they might need, or…"

"Or anything," Carley shrugged.

"Exactly," Laura said. "We didn't have a lot to go on. We don't have a lot to go on."

"But I bought the book here, from you, and I… we… were just hoping that there was some way that you could help us to help whoever left this book with you."

"Would you be able to give me the phone number?"

"Oh no, love. I couldn't possibly."

The woman looked at the two of them without speaking, and Laura was about to carry on talking, when Carley gave her a little nudge. She stopped and waited to hear what the woman would say.

"If I were to give you the address, you could give that to the police, couldn't you? Then they could do something. If they knew who it was and where they lived?"

The woman looked at them slyly, as though they were sharing the makings of a plan.

"Uh, yeah," Laura said. "We could do that."

Talking to the police again was the furthest thing from her thoughts. Her previous call was fruitless, and she wasn't about to go down that route again. What were the police going to do apart from telling her that there was no evidence that anyone needed any help?

"We would do that," Carley clarified.

"*We wouldn't*," Laura thought.

"I thought you didn't have the details here of who donated things to you?" Laura asked.

"Oh, we don't," the woman smiled, "But the Wexlers are regular donors. And buyers, come to think of it."

The Wexlers. That was a tremendous leap forward. The person who left the note had a name, and it was Wexler. Hearing it spoken aloud made the person seem more real. Rather than being the *idea* of a person writing a note asking for help, they were a living, breathing person that the person behind the counter of the shop, the person who was speaking to them now, had actually met.

"The Wexlers," Laura repeated, almost dreamlike.

"What are they like? The Wexlers?" Carley asked, with a more level-headed approach.

"Nice couple," the shop assistant said. "It's usually her that comes in, but the two of them are always full of smiles and chatter. Seems strange that either of them might ask for help."

Carley shrugged slightly. "You never know what's going on behind closed doors, I suppose," she said.

"Well, indeed," the shop worker said. "You hear about it all the time, don't you?"

Laura wasn't sure that she actually *did* hear about it all the time, but she had read enough books about secrets and lies. She knew that what you see on the outside can often not match up to what is actually happening in a relationship. She hadn't even realised what was happening in her own.

The woman picked up a piece of paper from the counter and pulled open a drawer, rummaging around for a pen. Finally, she pulled out a ballpoint, which also had the name of the shop and the red paw print logo printed along it.

"This is where they live," she said, scrawling an address on the scrappy paper. "Sue would probably kill me if she knew I was giving you this, so don't let on, will you?"

"Sue?" Laura asked.

"The woman who works on Mondays. She is one of those by-the-book types. Not buy-the-book, you know, *by-the-book*. Rules, rules, rules." She shook her head as though rules were the worst thing imaginable.

"I just hope the two of them are alright," she said. "Pop back in if you have a chance, and let me know what happens."

Carley took the piece of paper and nodded. She wasn't going to get caught up in a discussion about Sue and her troublesome adherence to privacy laws, that was for sure.

Laura craned to see what address was written on the paper, but Carley had already folded it up and put it in her pocket. It felt like Carley wanted to get out of the shop before the assistant had the chance to change her mind. Laura couldn't help but think that was a good idea.

"Thanks so much," Laura said, as Carley linked arms with her and hastened the two of them towards the exit.

"Yes. Thank you," Carley called over her shoulder.

It was only when they got out onto the pavement that the two of them spoke to each other.

"I can't believe it," Carley said in a high-pitched squeal. "Oh my… I guess it was Rules Rules Rules Sue that you talked to then. That girl. She couldn't wait to give us their details, could she?"

"She sounded like she knows this couple," Laura added. "Maybe she just wanted to help them. Or one of them."

Carley nodded and squeezed Laura tightly. "The Wexlers," she said, pulling the piece of paper back out of her pocket and opening it out. She read the address out loud. "46, Radley Street. I have no idea where that is, but we have Google Maps, and it can't be too far away if this is their local charity shop."

Laura bobbed her head. The excitement was overwhelming any sense of fear.

"We're really going, aren't we? We're almost there."

Carley agreed. "I know I said that we are past the point of no return, but if you have any doubts that we should go. I mean, if you think we should take this note to the police and let them deal with it…"

Laura paused for only a split second before deciding.

"We still don't have a lot to tell them. All we have is a note and an address that we've picked up from someone in a charity shop. And what if we get that girl in there in trouble?"

"We were lucky there, Laura," Carley said. "And I'm with you on this. Let's go and find out what's happening."

The thrill of the moment had taken over, and they were swept along in the current. The two of them bustled down the street, back towards Carley's car, and on to Radley Street.

CHAPTER NINETEEN

Once they had the address, finding the house was simple. Carley tapped the postcode into her phone and let the map come up with the route. It was a five-minute drive from the street she had parked on.

She slipped the car into gear and the two of them set off to finally reach their destination.

Before they had even arrived at the property, Laura was forming an impression of the area. The roads nearest to the charity shop had been red brick terraces, but as they headed along and off the main road, they turned onto an avenue boarded by grass verges to each side, with larger semi-detached houses.

Carley turned into Radley Street and said to Laura, "Watch out for number 46. That's 4, so it should be on your side."

"Okay," Laura tried to speak, but the word came out as a dry rasp.

"You all right?" Carley said.

"Yeah," Laura cleared her throat. "Well, you know. Wondering what's going to happen, but otherwise I'm all right."

"I am too," Carley said. "I know I might look like I'm being all confident and that, but I probably feel just the same as you."

"Stop," Laura said. "It's this one."

Carley pulled over, just ahead of the house they were looking for, far enough away to be out of view from the front windows of the building.

Once they had stopped, she turned to Laura.

"If you feel uncomfortable or worried at any time when we get there, just tell me, okay? And I'll do the same. We're here to help someone, but we need to look out for ourselves and each other, too."

"Yes, okay," Laura agreed. "Is it silly if we have a sign or something? Just in case?"

"Just in case of what?" she thought again for the second time that week.

"That's a good idea," Carley said. She thought for a second and then suggested, "Hold your hand like this." She made a loose fist and tucked her thumb between her first and middle fingers. "I used to have a habit of doing this when I was a kid. Drove my mum nuts for absolutely no idea that I could ever work out. Might come in useful now, though. It's not very obvious, and we'll know to look out for it."

Laura looked at Carley's hand and mimicked the action.

"Feels weird," she smiled. "But okay, that should work."

She took a couple of deep breaths, unconcerned by what Carley would think of this show of nervousness. They were in it together.

Carley extended out her arms in front of her, interlocking and stretching her fingers, as though she were warming up to play the piano. Then she dropped her hands onto her lap, relaxed.

"Ready?" she asked.

"As ready as I'm ever going to be," Laura said.

Carley gave a single nod and then pushed open the door and got out of the car.

Laura sucked in a final deep breath – in through the nose, out through the mouth – and joined her friend on the pavement.

They were finally standing outside number 46, at what they thought was the end of the trail.

Laura led the way, despite the deep churning in her gut. For a moment, before lifting the latch and pushing open the neat, white-painted gate, she let her hand pause. There was no going back, especially not now they were here, but what they were going to find going forwards and what they were going to do was all that she could think about.

The two women walked along the plain paving of the path and took in their surroundings as they went. The short-cropped, neatly cared for lawn was bordered by a frame of flower beds, bright with marigolds, gazanias and the bright pink and purple flourishes of fuchsias. It was an obviously well cared for garden, and as they walked along the path towards the house, Laura was already starting to form an impression of the kind of people that might live there. The Wexlers.

The house itself had a smart appearance. The front door was painted a bright postbox red, with a bright bronze lion head knocker and, to the side, a shiny matching doorbell.

Despite having no evidence to back up her assumption, apart from the smart-looking street upon which the property was situated, and the general feel of the house from the outside, Laura's mental image of the people that lived inside was one of a happy middle-class family. She would never have suspected that one of them might have needed help so badly that they left a note in a random book and sent it out into the world in a novel.

The women looked at each other and Carley reached her hand out to take Laura's and give it a gentle squeeze.

"Are you ready?" she said.

Laura nodded, then looked at the doorbell. No turning back.

Laura raised her finger to the button and pressed once, firmly. The doorbell sounded out in a heavy tone within the house. She was almost certain that her heartbeat was pounding out just as loud as the ringing. Again, she looked up at Carley.

This time, Carley didn't speak to reassure her. Her gaze was firmly fixed on the door, and all she could do to offer her support was to give a slight, forced smile. It was only at that moment that Laura realised Carley was just as scared as she was. Rather than fill her with dread, the idea that they were in it together, two women afraid, but feeling the fear and doing it anyway, somehow emboldened her. They were on the doorstep of a complete stranger because they had to be. Someone had asked for help, and they couldn't refuse. If the police weren't going to do anything, then maybe two Northern women with guts and determination would.

CHAPTER TWENTY

The wait for the door to be answered seemed never-ending. Laura and Carley stood on the path, unified in their tense anticipation. Laura could hear Carley's rapid, stuttering breathing, and it made her even more aware of her own. She was about to speak when she picked up the sound of footsteps from the other side of the door. It was the unmistakable noise of heels tapping on a wooden floor, and they were coming closer.

Laura straightened her posture, trying to make herself look as much like Confident Laura as possible. Carley followed her lead, and the pair stood and waited.

The door opened slowly, and there in front of them, at last, was the woman that they assumed to be Mrs Wexler.

"Hello?" the woman said, with an underlying waver of uncertainty.

A thought flashed through Laura's mind that the woman must be wondering what the two of them were selling, strangers, standing there on her doorstep.

Carley was craning her neck, trying to see into the house beyond, trying to see if anyone else was home, Laura supposed.

Laura took it upon herself to be the one to speak.

"Hi. I'm so sorry. You don't know us, but… we…" She lowered her voice. "We found something that we think might belong to you."

The woman frowned and looked from Laura to Carley and back again.

"To me? Are you sure?"

Laura felt a heavy ball in her stomach, a knot of uncertain fear and doubt.

She glanced over to Carley, and Carley nodded her head almost imperceptibly.

"I think so," Laura said. She reached into her bag and rummaged, trying to find the book. "I'm sorry. I thought I'd left it on top. I…"

"Do you think we could come in?" Carley asked.

"Are you selling something? You look a bit old to be girl guides, and I can't say I've ever seen double glazing hawkers that were quite as unprofessional as you before."

Laura's breath caught in her throat, and she felt the rising choke of anxiety.

Carley stepped in.

"We aren't selling anything. I know this is a bit weird…"

"A little, yes," the woman said.

"… but we've come from Yorkshire to find you. Laura…" She stopped, as though realising she wasn't starting at the right point in the story. "I sent a book to Laura. There's a group online where you can send a book to a stranger, and someone sends a book to you. Not the same person, like, someone else."

The woman in the doorway leant against the frame and regarded the two of them with a puzzled expression.

"I'm sorry. Let me get to the point."

"Please do," she said.

"Carley sent me this book," Laura said, finally producing it from her bag.

At this, the woman made her first visible reaction of recognition.

"Was this yours?"

The woman creased her brow and looked from Laura to Carley. "You said *she* sent it to you?" the woman said, sounding more confused than ever.

"Yes. She did," Laura said, trying to mask her exasperation. She wasn't doing well at getting her point across. She was terrible at speaking in front of other people. Ever since she had moved out of her marital home, it was as though she left her confidence behind.

"Then what has this got to do with me?" the woman asked.

"Was this your book?" Carley asked. Laura didn't know Carley well, but she knew enough to pick up the tension and frustration in her voice. She hoped that the woman in front of them wasn't so perceptive.

The awkwardness of standing on the stranger's doorstep whilst trying to explain what the two of them were doing there was heavy with anxiety. If they could sit down with her, perhaps they could talk. Maybe then she could tell them about the note. Laura was already starting to worry that this was the wrong woman, the wrong house, and not the person who they were looking for. On the other hand, there was the possibility that she wasn't in a position to talk to them and tell them what help she needed.

"Please. If you could let us sit with you, perhaps we can explain better."

"We've come all the way from Yorkshire," Laura said, a pleading edge creeping into her tone.

"Yorkshire? Well, that's a long way." She looked from Carley to Laura and back again, making a wordless assessment of them. "You'd better come inside," the woman said.

The two travellers followed her into the house, and she ushered them through into an airy lounge.

"Take a seat, please," she said. "My name is Melanie, by the way."

"Carley," Carley said, as Melanie waved her onto the sofa.

"And Laura. Hello. I'm sorry I'm such an idiot," she said.

"Not at all," Melanie said. "I'm not sure that I understand why you're here or what's happening. Perhaps you could explain again? Let me make some tea… or coffee? … then we can try to sort this out."

"Tea for me, please. Strong as you like."

"Same," Carley smiled.

As the woman turned to leave the room, Laura saw beyond her, through a white-painted set of French doors out into a leafy garden. On the patio was a cast iron table and chairs set, and sitting at that table, with his back to the house, was a dark-haired man. Laura tried not to stare, and noticed that, as Melanie left the room, she looked out at the man, before tossing a glance back towards her guests.

As soon as Melanie was out of earshot, Laura turned to Carley and moved her mouth close to her ear to whisper.

"Did she say it was her book or not? What's going on?"

Carley shrugged. "She didn't say it was, but then she didn't say it wasn't either. Although she looks a bit confused by it all."

Laura frowned and moved away. Then, thinking of something else she wanted to say, she hovered closer to Carley again.

"I've got a bad feeling about this," she said.

Carley said nothing, but nodded her head once. Melanie was coming back into the room, carrying a tray with their drinks on it.

"Here we go, ladies." She handed the cups to Laura and Melanie, and then sat down on the empty armchair, facing them.

"Thanks," the women said in unison.

"How sweet," Melanie said. "Now, tell me again what brings you here? Something about this book."

Laura had put the book down on the coffee table, and Melanie picked it up, turning it over in her hands, examining it as though it were a valuable artefact.

"Is it… I mean, *was it* yours?"

"It's not really the sort of thing that I read, to be perfectly honest. No offence intended, as I'm sure there's a market for this kind of…" She read the back of the book. "*Chilling domestic thriller.* What does that even mean? They all say that, don't they? The incredible twist that you'll never see coming. The unreliable narrator who is either drunk or quite, quite mad. Or isn't who you think they are in the first place. Yes, I read my share of these books when I was back in college. Not really my cup of tea now though," she said, picking up her actual cup of tea as she said it, as though trying to lighten the mood after her diatribe.

Laura spoke and her voice caught in her throat. She coughed gently and tried again. “What kind of books do you read, Melanie?”

“I don’t have all that much tome for reading now. I’m a fan of Ishiguro, if you’ve read any of his books?”

Laura was about to reply that yes, she had read several, and start off down the line of conversation that would have seen them talking about books for hours, rather than getting to the bottom of why she and Carley were both there.

Melanie was still holding the book, one hand gripping each side most unnaturally. She was studying it, moving it slowly up and down.

“Not really,” Laura lied. “So, you haven’t seen that book before?”

Melanie looked back down at the book as though she had forgotten that she was holding it.

“I can’t say that I have,” Melanie said. “It looks as though you’ve come all this way for nothing.”

"You see," Carley said, moving forward in her seat and sitting upright. "We got your address from the charity shop. Red Paw. Do you know it?" She didn't stop to wait for an answer. "And they said that this book was in a donation from this address."

"Well, I suppose there is no such thing as confidentiality anymore," Melanie huffed.

Without looking at Laura, Carley carried on talking. "So, you did donate it?"

"We send things to the charity shop all the time. Perhaps this got mixed in with some of the hand-me-downs and what-not."

Melanie placed the book back down on the table as though she no longer wanted to touch it. It had suddenly become toxic to her.

"I think you two had better tell me what all this is about."

Laura kept her voice quiet and low, so there was no risk of anyone else hearing her. "Melanie. We came because we got the note. We want to help you."

CHAPTER TWENTY-ONE

Melanie's first reaction when Laura mentioned the note was to look out into the garden, to where the man was sitting with his back to them. Laura shot a glance at Carley to see if she noticed; she did.

"The note," Melanie said, her voice calm and flat.

Laura kept her own voice quiet. "You did write it?"

"We haven't come to cause any trouble," Carley said. "And we don't want to make things… anything… difficult for you at all. We want to help."

"You have the note?" the woman asked. She shifted in her chair and put her mug down on the table next to her, almost as though she didn't feel safe to hold it.

Laura reached into the front pocket of her bag and brought out the piece of paper that had started this whole escapade. She leaned forward in her chair, stretching across the intricate rug on the floor between her and Melanie, and handed it to the woman.

Melanie held the edge of the paper gently.

"You got the note," she said, almost repeating herself.

"If there's anything at all…" Carley said. "Or if this isn't a good time, we could meet you somewhere? Talk somewhere private?" She looked beyond Melanie out into the garden as if signalling her recognition that the man was there, potentially able to hear them.

Melanie looked behind her, and then back at the women.

"Right," she said. "Yes, quite. That's Gerrard. He's always out there on the patio. Obsessed with getting his dose of vitamin D, you know?"

"Er…" Laura didn't know what so say, so she gave Melanie a friendly smile, and hoped that was answer enough.

"I should bring him in to meet you," Melanie said.

"You don't want to talk about this in private?" Carley asked, pointing at the note.

"What can I say?" Melanie spoke, her voice breaking. "It was a silly thing to do, leaving a note in a book like that. And now look, the two of you have somehow tracked the book down to us, to me, and you've come all this way." All the time as she spoke, Melanie was smiling in a way that appeared forced.

Laura frowned. She realised she was still sitting on the edge of her chair, but somehow couldn't bring herself to lean back and get comfortable. There was something discomfiting about the entire situation.

Either Melanie didn't want to talk about the note, or she couldn't talk about it. Carley had already offered to meet elsewhere, and Laura was out of ideas of what to suggest next. Their plan had been to play it by ear, but what they were hearing and seeing was proving difficult to decipher.

Carley seemed more determined.

"We couldn't just leave it," she said.

"No," said Melanie. "I suppose you couldn't." She turned the note over in her hand, as though looking for something else that might be written on the paper. Of course, there was nothing.

Carley extended her hand towards Melanie and placed it on her arm, stretching between the sofa and the chair in a bridge.

"We want to help, Melanie. That's why we came."

Melanie recoiled almost as soon as their skin touched.

"Oh, I'm sorry," Carley said, turning beetroot red and pulling herself backwards onto her seat. "I didn't mean to…"

"No, no. *I'm* sorry," Melanie replied. "I'm a little - what would you call it? - sensitive, sometimes."

Laura nodded. "It's okay. Please, it's fine. What Carley is trying to say is that we tracked you down because when I found the note, I couldn't imagine what it must have been like for the person who wrote it – for you. Having no one to talk to or reach out to. If the only help you could find was by writing this…" She gestured to the note. "… then I had to respond. We had to."

"Of course you did," Melanie murmured. She seemed more distant, less willing to talk, and Laura worried that Carley had done too much by trying to physically reassure her. A quick scan over her porcelain pale skin didn't show any evidence of bruises or other kinds of damage, but that didn't mean that there weren't any hidden beneath her draping black tunic or the smart beige cropped trousers she was wearing. Because she looked smart and stylish on the outside didn't mean that there wasn't something happening that she bore no signs of.

Melanie was as well presented as her spotless home, but Laura already knew, too well, that what a stranger saw wasn't necessarily the truth of the situation.

"Melanie," Carley said suddenly. Laura looked at her and followed her line of vision to the garden. Gerrard was standing up, looking into the house, watching the three of them.

CHAPTER TWENTY-TWO

Melanie's eyes flicked from Laura to Carley, and then she turned to look over her shoulder at the man in the garden.

"Oh," she said. Her voice was tight. "I should go and let him know who you are. He'll be worried. Would you excuse me a moment, please?"

"Are you sure?" Carley asked. "I mean, you could tell him we're…"

Melanie moved her head from side to side as she stood and walked towards the patio doors, but said nothing.

Laura and Carley were left holding their mugs of rapidly cooling tea, with nothing but questions.

"We need to get her alone somewhere," Carley said, keeping her voice as quiet as possible.

"What do you think's happening?" Laura asked. "The way she whipped her arm away when you touched her. Do you think…?" Laura didn't want to give voice to her fears, but the two of them both understood.

"I have no idea. It feels like she… I don't know how to describe it…"

"Like she feels bad about writing the note?"

"Yes!" Carley said, a little too loudly, and then had to put her hand over her mouth to keep her voice down. "Not like she regrets it, but… I don't know. Maybe she thinks she's wasted our time bringing us here."

"Because she can't talk about it now that we've come?"

"Whatever it is."

The women were building a picture of the situation from everything that had happened since they arrived at the house, but it was like putting together a jigsaw when they did not know what the final picture was supposed to look like. There were pieces here and there, and some of them fit together, but actually making out the overall image was impossible.

"So, what do we do?" Laura asked in a hissed whisper.

"What we've done so far," Carley said. "See what happens and go with it."

It was what they had done, that was true, but whether that plan was getting them anywhere was yet to be revealed.

The women's conversation was cut short as Melanie and Gerrard walked through the kitchen and into the lounge.

Melanie was smiling as they approached, and Laura wondered how much of it was for show.

"This is Laura and Charley," Melanie said, gesturing towards her guests.

"Carley," Carley said. Her voice sounded fragile, and she looked at Laura.

Laura tried to maintain an emotionless expression.

"Of course. Carley. Sorry." Melanie spoke without looking truly apologetic. "This is my husband, Gerrard," Melanie said.

"Hello ladies," Gerrard smiled. He didn't make any kind of move to shake their hands or approach them in any way. Instead, he stood stiffly by Melanie's side. In turn, she remained next to him, standing awkwardly rather than sitting back on the chair that she had been in minutes previously.

It was only then that Laura caught sight of the brown piece of paper on the table. The two words were visible, even from a couple of meters away, where she was sitting. Gerrard was standing much closer than that. He was going to see the note. He was going to find out that Melanie had written it. What she didn't know was how he was going to react.

Could she somehow get up, put something on top of the note to cover it? Swipe it off onto the floor without him noticing? Distract him and make him look somewhere else so that Carley could grab the note? Laura's brain cycled through different plans, all in a split second. The problem was that she was still looking at the note.

The real problem was that Gerrard noticed, and looked down at the table.

CHAPTER TWENTY-THREE

Laura almost let out a frustrated yelp as Gerrard leaned forward and picked up the paper. She stopped herself in the nick of time and instead forced herself to bite down on her lip to keep quiet. She felt Carley's hand tap against the side of her leg, but couldn't take her eyes off Gerrard now.

Gerrard held the paper up to the light, as though he was checking a banknote for a watermark.

"How fascinating," he said. He looked at the note, closer this time, examining it with forensic precision. "Quite amazing," he said.

It was far from the response that Laura had expected. Her stupor was broken as Melanie spoke.

"I told Gerrard about your note." Melanie remained standing close to her husband, looking up at him as she spoke.

He was about a foot taller than she was, but lean and toned. Although he was on the upper side of forty, he was a decent-looking man.

She told him? What had she told him? Clearly not that she had written it. Surely she wouldn't have admitted to that?

"What a darling little mystery," he said. The smile hadn't left his face. "Absolutely incredible."

His choice of words sounded peculiar. Perhaps that was how he always spoke. There was no way for Laura and Carley to know, but Gerrard seemed completely and unnaturally enthralled by the note.

He turned his gaze away from it to address the women. "And somehow you tracked this note down all the way from, where was it? Yorkshire? All the way from Yorkshire to our little home here. You've had a long, tiring journey, and it's such a shame that it's all been for nothing."

"But we…" Laura looked from Gerrard to Melanie, and then back to Carley. *All for nothing?* "We, er…"

"It's been quite an adventure," Carley said. She was far more quick-thinking than Laura, in the heat of the moment. Give Laura time and space and she could work out what to say, and how to do things, but under pressure, she cracked.

As she heard Carley speak, Laura could already tell that she had the makings of a plan. "We had to follow the note, of course."

"Of course," Gerrard said, still holding that same sardonic smile. There was something robotic about his expression, or perhaps it wasn't the face of a robot, but more that of a mannequin, fixed in an eternal, false smile.

"You know how I love little puzzles," Melanie said. Her voice was wavering, and Laura saw that Gerrard had reached his hand up behind her back. Was he supporting her, or was there something more malicious at play?

"It's certainly puzzling, isn't it, Mel?" he said, and Melanie twitched slightly.

Had he pinched her? Was he doing something behind her back? Laura couldn't see, and staring could only lead to things getting worse for Melanie. She was almost certain of that.

Whatever they had uncovered here, there was more going on than Melanie had been able to say.

"Well," Gerrard said, abruptly. "I'm sorry that we have wasted your time." He snapped his hand shut on the paper and crumpled it into a ball.

"Sorry," Melanie mouthed, without letting the sound escape.

"Right," Laura said.

"I got carried away," Melanie said. "I shouldn't have… well, leaving that note in the book was a stupid thing to do. Obviously, someone was going to find it and worry."

"You didn't realise that it would go to the charity shop though, did you, my love? If we had kept it right here, it would have stayed between us, our little game."

"It was a game? Between you two. Is that right?" Carley's voice surprised Laura as she spoke. "Melanie?"

"Yes!" Melanie said. "A little game. A puzzle. That's all. Nothing to worry about. I'm so sorry, honestly so sorry, that you have had to come all of this way."

She stepped away from Gerrard, and he gave her a swift look. Melanie reached down behind the sofa and Laura wondered what she was doing until she stood back up with her purse in her hand.

"Let me give you some money for the petrol. I feel terrible that you've wasted your time, and I know it's expensive these days."

"No, no." Carley waved away the two banknotes that Melanie was extending towards her. "We did what anyone would do. It's fine."

Laura wanted to ask more questions. Nothing that was happening made any kind of sense. Something was holding her back, and she let that gut feeling rein her in.

"Do you have somewhere to stay?" Gerrard asked. "Unfortunately, we don't have a guest room, or of course, we would offer our hospitality."

Melanie's expression wavered; Laura gulped. She couldn't imagine anything stranger than staying here with the Wexlers.

"We're in the Sunshine Hotel," Carley said. "Thanks though."

"Lovely place," Gerrard said. "Lovely. Or that's what I've heard. Well, can we at least offer you something to eat? Melanie was going to make, uh, pasta, I think. One of those…" He gesticulated as though waving his arms would help the women to understand what dish it was that his wife was planning to cook. It didn't help at all.

Still, Laura replied. "No. It's fine, really. But thanks. We've probably taken up enough of your time."

Whatever they were going to do next, she couldn't think of anything useful that they could achieve sitting in front of Gerrard. She started to rise to her feet, and Carley tapped her lightly.

"Would it be okay if I used your bathroom before we go, though, please?" Carley asked.

"Your hotel isn't far away," Melanie smiled.

Gerrard raised his hand to hush her. "Now, now, Mel. These ladies have had a long journey. I'm sure they're both feeling very disappointed and the least we can do is offer them the use of our bathroom. I assume you want to use the toilet and not take a shower or anything extravagant like that?" He grinned as though he had made the funniest quip imaginable.

In return, Carley smiled politely. "Just the loo, please," she said.

"'The loo'," Gerrard laughed. "Northern accents are so delightful. Go ahead. It's the room straight ahead of you when you get to the top of the stairs."

"Gerry, I…" Melanie said, seemingly not knowing how to finish her sentence.

Again, her husband batted her words away.

"Go ahead. Now, do you need a top up there while you wait for your friend?" He nodded towards her mug, which she had hardly drunk from before the contents had gone cold.

"Uh, it's…" Laura tried to turn down the offer, but Gerrard had already tapped Melanie on the shoulder, which was seemingly her cue to head off into the kitchen and bring the drink she hadn't asked for.

Carley threw a look in Laura's direction, which Laura interpreted as meaning something along the lines of *I don't want to leave you with him, but I really need to use the bathroom*.

Laura gave her a small nod and watched as she left the room and headed for the stairs.

"Straight ahead at the top," Melanie called from the kitchen.

"Straight on. Got it," Carley shouted back. By the sound of her footfalls on the stairs, she was already halfway up.

Laura was almost certain that there was something very strange going on, but she couldn't work out what it was. From the jumbled thoughts she was trying to piece together, she cobbled a plan. Have the drink, wait for Carley, and get the hell out of there. It seemed like a decent plan, whatever was happening.

Gerrard slithered around the armchair and sat down, facing Laura.

"What is it you do, Laura?" he asked. It was a perfectly normal question, but something about the way that he asked made her skin crawl.

"I…" She was about to say that she was taking some time off work, staying at home with her mother, but being entirely truthful felt out of place. "I'm an estate agent," she said instead. It was the truth for a version of her, the version that she wanted to be at that moment in time. When she was an estate agent, she was

Confident Laura. She needed to be Confident Laura in front of this man.

"So, you must spend a lot of time snooping around other people's houses," he deadpanned.

Laura spluttered, her words catching in her mouth, and she could feel her cheeks heating with a rush of blood.

Gerrard let out a hooting laugh that made her recoil before she could moderate her response.

"Only joking, my dear," he said. "But isn't that the fun part of it? You get to see what's happening in other people's lives? It must be fascinating, quite fascinating."

"I… I like my job," she stuttered. It was true, and thinking about it, sitting there hundreds of miles from home, in a stranger's home under peculiar circumstances, Laura wished she was instead at her desk at Chaucer and Sons. She wished that the person who she was presenting as to Gerrard was the person who she still was in reality.

"That's great, Laura," he said, though his cold, emotionless voice didn't match his sentiment.

"We have quite a lovely home here, you must admit," he said, waving his hand as though showing off the property. "And we are very happy here."

Laura felt the already tense atmosphere tighten further.

"We are very happy," he repeated, and leaned forwards towards Laura.

With his face only inches from hers, he spoke again. "You should go home and forget all about the note. You've had a little holiday, spent some time away from home, and now it's time to go back and get on with your own little lives."

There were the slightest hints of coffee on his breath, and it was warm against her skin. Laura wanted to pull back, but instead she sat her ground.

"Do we have an understanding?" he asked.

Is Melanie okay? she wanted to ask. The words were there, on the tip of her tongue, almost begging to be let out. Instead, she looked beyond Gerrard, into the kitchen where she could see the woman standing, leaning against the kitchen counter, her back to the two of them, not making their drinks, just standing, leaning, lost in her own thoughts.

"She is fine. We are fine," Gerrard said, as though reading the thoughts that Laura hadn't spoken.

Laura turned her eyes back to the man, still in her personal space, too close, too intimate.

"Everything all right?"

It was Carley.

Gerrard didn't leap back into his chair when Carley spoke. Instead, he lingered a couple of seconds longer, there directly in front of Laura, looking into her eyes.

Carley stood in the doorway, and ran her own eyes over Laura, remembering the sign they had agreed on should either of them need help. Either Laura had forgotten it, or she didn't need Carley to step in, as her hands were on her lap, wavering slightly, but otherwise flat.

Slowly, Gerrard moved back into the armchair, and finally spoke as though Carley's words had only just reached him.

"We are fine," he said again, both answering Carley's question and reaffirming what he had told Laura.

"Right," said Carley. "Well, we'll be going then." She didn't re-enter the room, but stood instead, waiting for Laura to get up and join her.

Laura got to her feet, not taking her eyes off Gerrard, and stood momentarily before walking over to where her friend was standing.

When she reached Carley, she shot one final glance into the kitchen. Melanie was still propped against the counter. She wished she could say something else to her, let her know how she could get in touch with them if she wanted to or needed to, but there was no way that she could think of to do that.

Carley motioned towards the front door with a swift movement of her head.

"Let's go," she said.

"Thank you so much for taking the time to visit," Gerrard said. "It's reassuring to know that there are such *good* people in the world." He stressed the word good as though it was an insult rather than a compliment.

"Sure," Carley said, before reaching for Laura's arm, looping it and pulling her forwards and out of the house.

When they were in the garden and back on the path, Laura let go of Carley and started wiping herself down with her hands.

"I feel dirty," she said. "I know their house was absolutely spotless, but I feel like I've got him all over me."

"Did he touch you?" Carley stopped in her tracks, so suddenly that Laura walked into the back of her.

"No!" Laura yelped in revulsion. "Gosh, no! Just the way he was looking at me. Not only that though, I mean there was something about the whole place that made me feel… I don't know, it gave me the creeps."

Carley's eyes drifted from her friend to the front window of the house. Gerrard and Melanie were standing, she with his arm around her shoulder, both staring at them. When Melanie saw Carley looking, she raised one hand and gave a tiny wave. Gerrard did nothing. He stood, watching.

"Let's get the heck out of here," Carley said, tugging at Laura's sleeve and hurrying her down along the path and out of the garden.

CHAPTER TWENTY-FOUR

The walk back to the car took less than a minute, but felt like an eternity to the two women. Laura pulled open the door and flopped into the passenger seat, confused and feeling defeated.

Carley didn't start the engine immediately.

"What was he saying to you?" she asked.

"Something about their lovely house and their lovely lives and how we should forget about the note and leave them alone," Laura said, trying to remember Gerrard's exact words. She could still feel that warm coffee breath against her face, and wanted to shower, scrub at her skin and remove every trace of him.

"He was all up in your face. It looked weird."

"It felt weird. There's something not right about him, that's for sure. But what can we do?"

Carley shrugged. "Melanie could have said something, surely. When we were alone. Or she could have given us some sort of sign?"

"I guess," Laura said. "Maybe that's how it works in books, but when you're the one in an unpleasant situation, maybe you don't think about things like that. Perhaps the only thing she could think about was acting normally, whatever that is for those two, in front of her husband. If she really needs help, it might not be the sort of thing she can talk about when he's there."

Carley listened and then slammed her hands on the dashboard.

"Damn it," she said. "Damn, damn, damn." She slapped the dashboard three times as she barked the words.

Laura was wordless, looking on, not knowing what to say.

Carley glanced into the rear-view mirror, wiped her hair from her face and straightened herself up in her seat. Then, without speaking further, she slipped the car into gear, and they drove away from Radley Street in silence.

It was a long ten minutes in the car without conversation. There had barely been a lapse in chatter between the women since they had met, but now the two of them were caught up in their own thoughts.

They got out of the car and made their way back up to their room, and only then did one of them speak.

"Laura, I've thought it over all the way back here." Laura sat on the edge of her bed, waiting to hear Carley's plan. Instead, she was disappointed to hear her say, "I have absolutely no idea what we should do now."

"Something's not right, and I can't put my finger on exactly what it is," Laura said.

It was as though there was a something stuck beneath her skin that was irritating her, but she couldn't get at it to dig it out.

"Too right," Carley agreed. "That guy is a creep. Whatever she needs help from, it obviously involves him. Ugh. But what do we do?"

Laura pursed her lips. "It's something else. I know what you're saying about him, but…" She looked Carley dead in the eyes. "Isn't there something off about her, too? That's not what's bugging me though, do you know what I mean?"

"If he's doing something to her, then maybe she was just scared. Perhaps she couldn't talk with us there, or…"

Laura shook her head, irritated. "When we first arrived, she was on her own with us. He couldn't have heard her from where he was, out there in the garden. The windows were closed, he had his back to us."

"Unless he's monitoring the house. He could have some kind of device. A baby monitor or…"

"Just in case someone goes around to talk to his wife? And wouldn't we have seen something? I saw you having a good look around, and you know that I did, too."

Carley smiled at that comment. "Of course we did."

"Right then. Unless it were hidden away, and what reason would he have to hide something in his own house?"

Carley let out an exasperated wail. "Then what is it, and what do we do now?"

"I'm not saying that this is what we *should* do, but what do you think about going back to the police? We have a lot more information that we could give them now. Maybe it's time to let them take over."

Carley thought about this for a few moments before replying. "Do you not think that they would do pretty much what we've done? Go round there, ask a few questions, hear Melanie telling them that everything is fine?"

"They probably deal with domestic cases like that all the time, though. They'd know what to do?"

Carley nodded. "Sure, they'd leave them to it, and Melanie would probably be in all kinds of trouble with her husband. If we've not already caused that by going round there today. If he's as bad as we think he is, maybe going to the police is only going to make things worse. If she wanted the police to help her, wouldn't she have phoned them rather than leaving that note?"

"The note!" Laura yelped. "He took the note. We don't even have that anymore. We haven't got anything to show the police, even if we went back to them."

She flopped backwards onto the bed and kicked her legs in frustration.

Meanwhile, Carley remained upright, sitting on her own bed, deep in thought.

They had travelled a hundred and fifty miles to be there, spent the night in this decidedly average hotel, and so far, they had achieved nothing. Tomorrow they were due to check out and go home, back to their normal, everyday lives.

"Can we really leave it like this?" Carley asked, almost rhetorically. "We came to help whoever wrote the note, and I don't know about you, but I don't think that we've done that."

Laura was still on her back, but she had stopped kicking and was instead staring at the white-painted ceiling, trying to make sense of the day.

"No, I don't either," she said. She rolled onto her side so that she could look at Carley.

"Do you have to be home tomorrow?" Carley asked. There was a slight change in her tone, and Laura picked up on it in a flash.

"Have you got a plan?" Laura asked, propping her head up onto her hand, eager to hear what Carley had to say. "All that's waiting for me at home is my mum, who

I really should message now because she's probably worried to death about me, and endless hours of daytime television."

She made a mental note to call her mum as soon as she and Carley had finished speaking.

"What would you think about staying on an extra day? We could wait until Gerrard leaves the house and go and talk to Melanie alone? At least we would know then, for sure."

"We'd have given her every opportunity to tell us what's happening and ask for help if she wants it," Laura agreed. "Without *him* around."

Carley let an exaggerated shudder ripple through her body.

"Brrr!" she said emphatically. "I don't think I could bear to be near him again."

"So, what are we going to do? Sit outside their house and wait for him to leave? We could be there all day."

"Well, we have each other," Carley said. Then she reached over to the bedside table and picked up her Kindle. "And we have books."

Laura raised the corners of her mouth into a smile. “We always have books,” she agreed.

“It’s hardly a high-tension police stake-out, but I think it’s the only plan we have now.”

“Whatever happens, at least we’ll know that we tried everything.”

Carley nodded. “It’s a plan,” she said.

“It’s a plan,” Laura repeated.

She reached up and raised her hand for a high five. The disappointment of the day was fading into hope for what they might achieve the following day.

All they could do was try. If Melanie needed their help, they had to do as much as they could to give it. Whatever it took.

CHAPTER TWENTY-FIVE

The following morning, Carley and Laura were parked up on Radley Street. Laura had experienced another night of broken sleep, but the adrenaline of executing their plan was driving her forwards. The women sat in tense silence, taking turns to read a few pages of their books and then survey the house for signs of Gerrard leaving.

Laura's phone cut the atmosphere with a harsh ringing trill, and she dropped her Kindle onto her lap, barely stopping it from falling onto the floor.

She pulled her phone out of her bag and looked at the screen. It was Jamie.

As soon as she saw his name, it hit her. She was meant to be meeting with the solicitor. The appointment was for eleven o'clock, and it was twenty past already. She had become so accustomed to having no plans for any given day that she'd forgotten about the one appointment she had made.

She had ignored so many of his calls, and now was a perfect time to continue that, but Carley saw her phone screen and nodded.

"Talk to him," she said. "Avoiding it will never help you."

Laura sighed. Carley was right, and she knew it.

"I'll keep watch," Carley offered.

Laura accepted with a dip of the head and clicked to take the call.

"Jamie!" Laura tried to keep her voice calm and controlled, but it still sounded tense as she spoke.

"Where are you? What the hell have you got yourself into?"

Brilliant, she thought. I'm sitting outside a stranger's house, two hours away from home, and when I thought it couldn't get any worse, there he is, reminding me of everything that's going wrong in my life.

"What do you want?"

"I spoke to Catharine," he said. "What are you doing? This is crazy. It's not like you at all."

Well, that's something. I'm sure there's a compliment hidden in there.

"If you've spoken to Mum, I'm sure you already know everything there is to know about where I am and what I'm doing. In case you hadn't noticed, we are living our own lives now. Alone."

Back at home, Laura would have looked up to her mother for moral support as she spoke. Now she looked at Carley, who was half-looking at her in a way that suggested she didn't know if she was meant to be listening in.

Part of her was annoyed that her mum had told Jamie where she was, and what she was doing, but she knew Catharine would only have told Jamie the minimum, and that she would have done it with the intent of caring for her.

"Who is this woman you're with? And what are you doing in Cambridge?"

Maybe he didn't know as much as he thought he did.

"Look, I'm busy now. With my friend," Laura said, looking at Carley again.

"This isn't like you," he said. "You don't just go racing off down the country with a stranger."

Of course, he wouldn't know that she had missed the appointment with the solicitor. How could he? Laura's mind had put two and two together and made at least seven. That's how effective it was at over-thinking. She would call them and rearrange, tell them that something had come up, and she would make sure that she kept the appointment. Who was Jamie to tell her what she was like, or what she could or couldn't do?

He hadn't been a controlling partner, or an abusive husband. Everything had been smooth sailing between them, right up until the point that they had run aground. But now, she was responsible for her own life and her own decisions, no matter how questionable they might currently be.

"Perhaps you just don't know me anymore," Laura said with calm confidence that she barely recognised.

The line was silent at Jamie's end.

"Is that everything?" Laura asked.

"How did this happen to us?" Jamie asked, his voice quieter and softer than Laura had heard it since their separation.

It was a question that she had asked herself countless times since Jamie had told her he wanted to end their marriage. How did it happen?

"People change," she said. "And sometimes people stay the same, but we realise we never really knew them in the first place."

"And which of those things happened to us?" he asked, as though genuinely looking for the answer.

"I don't know," she said. "But I think I am changing now. And I think it's for the better."

Again, there was a moment of silence before Jamie spoke.

"Good," he said. With no hint of malice, he added, "I want you to be happy, Laura. Whatever happens."

There was something different about this conversation that she was unprepared for. She didn't know how to reply because she didn't expect the words that she was hearing from her husband. All she could think of to say was, "Okay. Thank you."

Carley gave her a quizzical look and went back to looking at the house.

"Hey," Carley nudged Laura. "It's Gerrard. He's going."

Laura was relieved that she had a reason to end the call to Jamie, even if that meant that she was about to go back to the Wexler's house.

This time, without Gerrard present, perhaps they could really help Melanie.

The women watched as Gerrard stepped into a smart and rather expensive-looking black car and drove off away from them.

"This is it," Laura said.

"Let's go," Carley agreed.

They climbed onto the pavement, and walked, hurried by the urgency of the situation, back to the little white gate and the path to number forty-six.

When they reached the doorstep, Laura and Carley stood so they couldn't be seen from the front window before pressing the doorbell.

The chime echoed into the hall, and this time Laura could imagine Melanie inside, going about whatever she did when her husband wasn't around, hearing the bell, walking towards the door.

The actual series of events took longer that than, and the women looked at each other. Carley rang the buzzer again.

"Maybe she isn't home either," Carley said. "She might have gone out before we got here."

"I didn't think of that," Laura said. "What if she…"

But her sentence was cut off as they heard the same heels clicking on the polished floor that they recognised from the previous day. Melanie pulled the door open and greeted them with a perplexed expression.

"You again?" she said as she saw the women.

"We couldn't just leave without having the chance to talk to you alone," Laura said.

"Alone?" Melanie repeated.

"We saw your husband, Gerrard. We saw him leave." Carley chipped in to explain.

Melanie tilted her head to the side.

"Have you been watching us? You've been *spying* on our house?"

It seemed a strange choice of words from someone that had asked for help.

"Can we come in?" Carley asked for the second day in a row.

"I'm not sure that's necessary," Melanie said.

"But he isn't here. You can talk to us now."

"We really do want to help you," Laura added.

"Then the best thing you can do is turn around, walk back down my path, leave and never come here again." Melanie's voice was hard and cold as ice.

The women looked at each other.

"But…" Laura began.

"I don't need your help, okay? I don't want you here, and neither does anyone else. If you keep coming back, you're going to find yourself in a situation that you really don't want to be in. Do we understand each other?"

This wasn't the sound of someone who had written a plea for help and had left it in a book for a stranger to find. This was someone who had something to hide. Laura was sure of it.

"Gerrard?" she asked a question, just by suggesting his name.

Melanie looked confused for a second, and then let out a shrill laugh.

"Him?" Her laughter didn't stop. "You think *he* needs help? Darling, you have absolutely no idea what you are doing here, and you seem to have no ability to read a situation. Maybe thrillers aren't for you? Perhaps get yourself a little rom-com chick lit girlie book and stick with those."

Laura's face reddened, and her tongue tightened in her mouth.

"Listen, Melanie. We came all this way to help you," Carley took over. "There's no need to be rude. If you don't want our help, fine, but this all seems…" she trailed off. "Right," she said. "Yes, we'll go."

Laura gave her a quizzical look. She had started off defending her, and now she was giving up and retreating. Whatever Laura knew about Carley, she didn't think she was someone that would throw in the towel like that. If she was backing down, there was a reason.

"Come on," Carley said, pulling Laura gently. "I'm sorry to have taken up your time, Melanie."

"Please don't presume to take up any more of it," Melanie said. "Forget about my silly little note now. I am fine. Gerrard is fine. We don't need you, and I certainly don't want you here."

"Message received," Carley said. "I've heard you loud and clear."

Laura didn't have a chance to say anything else, and wouldn't have known what to add, anyway. Carley almost frog-marched her down through the garden and out onto the pavement. They hurried back to the car, got in, and sat, almost panting, with the total rush of the past few minutes.

"Are you going to tell me what the heck is going on?" Laura said once she was sitting in the passenger seat.

"We missed a vital clue," Carley said. "Or a couple of clues, now I think of it. You know when you're reading a book and one character says something that seems innocent at the time, but then you go back over it and think, 'hey wait a minute'?"

Laura bobbed her head in acknowledgement.

"Well…" Carley said and waved her hand over towards the house. "That's exactly what happened just now."

CHAPTER TWENTY-SIX

Laura wracked her brain, trying to work out what she had missed. When she was reading, she could spot the plot twists coming in almost every book she read. She would have said that picking up on clues and unravelling puzzles was one of her skills, but that was fiction, and this was real life.

"So, what was it?" Laura asked. Her voice was high-pitched and urgent.

Carley turned sideways in her seat, as far as the steering wheel would let her, to face Laura.

"Okay, well, there are a couple of things. Maybe a few things. When Melanie was talking just then, she said that she didn't want us there, and neither did *anyone* else. Not neither did *Gerrard*, but neither did *anyone*."

Carley was animated, her eyes wide with excitement. Laura, on the other hand, was trying to work out exactly what she was saying.

"So…" She tried to look as though she understood, but Carley had obviously made a breakthrough that she was still finding it difficult to make sense of.

"Well, I might have thought nothing of that, but… do you remember yesterday when we first came here?"

"Of course."

Carley hadn't finished speaking. "Of course," she said. "But when Gerrard asked whether we had somewhere to stay, he said that they didn't have a guest room."

"Okay…" Laura listened for further explanation.

"But when I went up to the loo, there were two other doors off the landing. One must have been their bedroom, but the other…"

"Could have been a cupboard?"

"Look," Carley pointed at the house. The downstairs window was obscured by the hedge, but Laura could clearly see the gate, the path and the upstairs windows.

"There are two windows across the front there," Carley said. "The bathroom is at the back of the house."

"You're saying that they *do* have another bedroom?"

"And if they have another room, but they don't have a guest room, they are using it for something."

She paused and looked at Laura to see if she had caught up and made the connection.

"Don't you see? There's someone else living there. And I bet that whoever is living with them is the person who wrote the note. It's not Melanie that needs help."

"There's someone else." Laura repeated the words as the jigsaw pieces started to fall into place. "That's why she told Gerrard about the note. She wasn't scared of him finding out. She wanted us to know."

"They wanted us out of there. Remember how clear Melanie was about me going straight into the bathroom?"

"Top of the stairs," Laura recalled.

Carley nodded excitedly and grabbed Laura's hands.

"We're finally getting somewhere. This all makes sense, don't you think? Tell me if you think I'm wrong, or if I'm nuts."

"I think you could be right," Laura said, thinking back over everything that

Melanie and Gerrard had said and done. "He wanted to destroy the note. If he was abusing Melanie, surely he would use it, you know, keep it to use against her…"

Carley shrugged. "Maybe, but I think the fact that he wasn't angry about it…"

"There was something though, wasn't there? He wasn't angry, but he was definitely annoyed."

"They want us out of the way, keeping our nose out of it. But there's someone in that house that needs help."

"If Melanie had pretended she was the one that needed our help, they could probably have got us to stop snooping around."

"I guess she just didn't think of that. I don't expect they ever thought that anyone would be onto them."

There was a moment of silence before Laura asked the question that she couldn't answer and couldn't shake from her mind.

"So… if there's someone there that needs help, who is it?"

"And what are Melanie and Gerrard doing to them?"

Although the car windows were closed, a chill air swept over the women.

Laura swallowed and spoke, her voice quavering. "It must be a child. Their child."

Carley's face was ashen. "We've got to do something, and we've got to act fast. If they have a child shut away up there that needs our help, it's probably only got worse for them since Melanie and Gerrard found out about the note."

"Oh, what have we done? We might have caused all kinds of trouble. All I wanted to do was help, and look what's happening."

"Gerrard is out of the house. Melanie is on her own in there… well, apart from the person we need to help. Between us, do you think we could get into the house, distract her, and get upstairs?"

The situation had spiralled more quickly than Laura could ever have imagined. Her heart was beating out of her chest, and she tried her best to take the calming breaths she had never quite got the hang of.

"It's in through the nose and out through the mouth," Carley said with a slight smile. "Does it help?"

Laura kept taking the breaths and shook her head. "Not really."

With that, Carley managed to find a laugh, despite the tension in the air.

"Look, we can do this. We'll go back to the house. Get inside. I'll distract Melanie, and you run upstairs, okay?"

Laura acknowledged with a bob of her head. She was much happier with the task of running up to find the person upstairs rather than being left with Melanie.

"And then what?"

"Let's get them out of there. Once we find out what's going on, we can decide what to do next."

"The police?"

Carley shrugged her shoulders. "Depends what's happening, I suppose. And it depends what we find."

Laura had already painted a mental image of a child stuck in their room, held prisoner by their wicked parents. In fact, she imagined the child was a teenage girl. There were no grounds for that thought, and perhaps her preconception came from the books she had read or stories she had seen on the news. There was no point in speculating. What was important was that they had to do something, no matter who it was that needed their help.

CHAPTER TWENTY-SEVEN

For the second time that day, Laura and Carley stood on the doorstep of the Wexlers' house.

Laura rang the doorbell and again they waited for the clacking of heels in the hall. It didn't take long for the sound to ring out.

Melanie opened the door, but as soon as she saw who was standing on the step, she tried to push it closed again.

"Go away," she said. "Did you not get the message last time?"

Laura pushed back against the door and tried to stop Melanie from closing it.

"Move!" Melanie barked. "I don't want anyone to get hurt here. Just, please, leave me alone. Go away. Go home."

Laura and Carley pushed at their side of the door and Melanie shoved on the other. This wasn't the clean 'get back inside and distract her' that either of them had imagined.

Melanie gave a mighty shove, and before the friends could gain traction, the door slammed in their faces.

"Two against one and she's stronger than us?" Carley said with a huff.

Laura lowered her head. "I'm so useless," she muttered under her breath.

"There's no time for feeling sorry for ourselves, Laura," Carley said, jabbing her lightly. "Come on."

Carley set off down the path, and Laura watched for a split second before lolloping after her.

"Where are we going? We can't just leave."

"We're not," Carley said. "But another thing I remembered was those lovely patio doors. Let's slip around the back and see if we can get in there."

Laura marvelled at Carley's ability to pick up on every detail, and wished she had the same mental acuity. The months of sitting at home, watching daytime television, had seemingly dulled her once sharp mind. Even though she had only played at being Confident Laura, that version of herself had been snappy and sharp. She was letting herself deteriorate the longer she moped and moaned around her mum's house.

"This is it," she said, coming to a stop by the rear gate. "Look." She pointed through to the patio set they had seen Gerrard sitting on the previous day. It seemed such a long time ago, and yet it had been less than twenty-four hours.

"That's it," Laura agreed.

"I can't see Melanie," Carley said. "Can you?"

Laura shook her head. "I hope that means that she can't see us either."

Carley pushed at the gate, but it didn't move. She gave a little more pressure, shoving at it with her shoulder, as they had tried to do with the front door. Still, nothing happened.

"Locked?" Laura asked.

They looked over the gate. There was no obvious locking mechanism.

"Bolted on the other side, maybe?" Carley suggested.

Then she turned to Laura. "I'm going to give you a leg up. Think you can climb over. If there's a bolt, you can let me in."

Laura was about to suggest that Carley be the one to climb over instead, but she stopped herself. Confident Laura would have done this. She would have forced herself to take the lead and accept the task.

"Okay, let's do it," she said.

They had both seen this done in films, but it was the first time that either of them had needed to do it in real life.

Carley formed a step out of her hands, cupping them together.

"I think you're meant to stand there, and then I somehow boost you up," Carley said, her tone speculative.

"Well, we'll find out," Laura said.

She stepped forward, put one foot into Carley's hands, and reached up for the top of the gate. It was a good six feet tall, she estimated, as it towered above the two of them. Still, she grabbed hold of the top, and as Carley grunted and lifted her, she pulled herself for all she was worth.

"Remember why we're doing this," she told herself out loud.

"You up?" Carley said, her breath showing the strain of holding Laura's weight.

Laura hefted herself upwards, her legs kicking behind her, and clumsily got to the top of the gate.

"Yes!" she exclaimed. Her voice did not conceal the sense of triumph she felt at this minor achievement. Her joy was squashed as she tumbled over the other side of the gate and fell in a heap onto the gravel path beyond. "Ugh!" she yelped.

"You okay? Laura?" Carley was trying to keep her voice down again. Their stealth mission to enter the house from the rear would be for nothing if Melanie heard them and locked the patio doors before they got inside.

"I'm alright," Laura said. She stood and brushed herself down. Her leg had collided with a small decorative boulder set to the side of the path as she landed, and she knew already that the purple bloom of a bruise would be starting to form there. Still, she rubbed at it, and told herself that there was no time to worry about it now.

Laura scrambled to her feet and stood behind the gate that separated her from her friend.

"The patio door is open," Laura said in a hushed whisper. "Come on, let's get you in."

She pulled at the bolt, and it moved stiffly across, allowing the garden gate to be opened.

Carley greeted Laura with a wide grin. “Well done, Laura,” she said. “I’d never have got over there.”

The two friends stood at the bottom of the long, beautifully landscaped garden, looking up at the house.

“Whatever happens, you get upstairs, okay?” Carley said, her expression now deadly serious.

“I will. I’ll be quick,” Laura said. “And you be careful.”

Carley responded with a single nod of her head.

“Come on,” she said.

Laura stepped forward and led the way along the gravel path up to the patio and to the door that would take them into number 46, Radley Street.

Laura stood at the open patio door, looking into the house, trying to see where Melanie was. From where she was standing, she had a clear view of the lounge, and realised that this was only feet away from where Gerrard had been standing the previous day when she and Carley had first visited.

They stood to the side of the door, trying to keep out of any likely line of vision, listening for the sound of the woman that had sent them away from the house, looking out for any sign of Melanie.

The kitchen was empty. The kitchen was spotless, the counters showroom clean and not a utensil out of place. She remembered a kitsch sign that she had once read, something about a tidy kitchen being the sign of a dull mind. Whether that was true, she thought there was definitely something not quite right about a house that was so perfectly maintained. Not that she was untidy; she was what she liked to think of as normal.

"Nice," Carley whispered. "Everything is just so… nice."

"She's in the lounge there." Laura spoke only loudly enough for Carley to hear her and pointed through to the back of Melanie's head. She was sitting in the same armchair that Gerrard had leaned forward in the previous day, and Laura felt a shudder run through her body at the thought of him.

The route to the hallway and on to the stairs would take Laura through the kitchen, and as long as she was quiet, would not attract Melanie's attention.

"I'll go on ahead," Laura said. She hadn't planned to take the lead, but now they were at the door, it was starting to come naturally to her. Her instincts were taking over, adrenaline fuelling her onwards.

"Okay," Carley said, also careful to keep her voice low. The last thing they wanted was for Melanie to spot them now and stop them from getting into the house and up to the person who needed them. Rather than elaborate on the plan, Carley looked at Laura, waiting to be told what to do.

"Stay down here, and if you see Melanie heading for the stairs, do whatever you can to distract her." Laura didn't know what Carley could do, but what she did know was that Carley would think of something.

Carley didn't ask what that something was, either. Instead, she agreed. "I'll be here. And if you need me, you shout, and I'll be up there with you, okay?"

"Okay," Laura replied.

With that, she stepped through the open patio door, onto the slate tile of the kitchen floor. Her shoes were not the same hard click-clacking heels that Melanie wore, and she was, for once, glad of her simple footwear. Her trainers allowed her to tread almost silently across the hard floor. Although she was almost certain that her heart was pounding loudly enough for Melanie to hear it, Laura made her way stealthily through the room and on into the hallway beyond.

The slate tiles gave way to polished parquet, and after only a few steps on the hard wood, Laura found herself at the bottom of the staircase.

Looking up the stairs, they may as well have been a mountain that she was about to climb. She had the same sense of apprehension: the danger of the climb, and the uncertainty about what she would find when she reached the summit. At the top of the stairs, she was going to have to summon all the emotional strength she had to open the door and face whoever was inside. Laura knew she needed to stay calm so that she could do what she and Carley had travelled all the way here for – to help the person who had written the note.

The staircase itself was carpeted in a thin, expensive-looking, colourful weave. There were little silver bars set back on each step, holding the carpet in place. Everything about this house was elegant, and much as she disliked the people who lived here, she couldn't fault their sense of taste. It seemed terribly unfair that such bad people could have such good things, whilst all she had was her childhood bedroom in her mother's house.

What would Catharine think if she could see her now? Laura paused at the bottom of the stairs, considering the question. Would she encourage her to carry on, get to that room and rescue its inhabitant, or would she tell her to be careful, get out of there and phone the police instead?

She heard Catharine's voice echoing inside her head.

This is not just silly, it's dangerous.

And then:

I want you to be happy again, but more than that, I want you to be safe.

What would happen to her mum if anything happened to her? How would Catharine feel if she walked up these stairs and found more that she could handle?

I want you to be safe.

The words reverberated around her mind. Before taking another step forward, Laura reached into her pocket and took out her phone. She flicked the switch on the side to silent, making sure that no noise from the device would be able to attract any attention, and then she typed a message to her mum.

I'm at the house. 46, Radley Street. I'm safe, but if anything happens to me, that's where I am.

Laura stared at the screen. Her mum was likely to be more worried than reassured by the message. In fact, she herself was worried by it. Sending her mum the address meant that she was acknowledging that the next few minutes could be dangerous.

I'll text you later. I love you.

Laura added the last words and then clicked *send*.

Then she slipped the phone back into her pocket, turned her eyes upwards, and walked up the stairs.

CHAPTER TWENTY-EIGHT

Laura stepped slowly onto each stair as she climbed. It reminded her of when she was a teenager, coming home after curfew and creeping into her bedroom after a night out with her friends. The difference was that back then, she knew which steps creaked, and where she should avoid treading. Now, she gingerly let her weight fall onto each step in turn, fearful with every move forward that Melanie would hear her and race up the stairs to apprehend her before she reached her goal.

There was no noise from the wood beneath the extravagant carpet, though, and better still, no noise from downstairs.

Even with the slow progress that came from her covert approach, Laura made her way to the top of the staircase in no time. Directly in front of her was the bathroom, so the room she was looking for was behind one of the other two doors on the landing. Both were white-painted wood, and both were closed.

Laura looked from one to the other and what she saw gave her no indication of which one she should approach. She moved forward, and pressed her each against the cold, smooth wood.

The muffled echo of the room filled her ear. No speech. No music. No movement that she could discern. Laura closed her eyes tightly, focusing on any minute sound she might be able to hear.

"Hello? Are you there?" she whispered, not wanting to alert Melanie to her presence, but at the same time, trying to get the attention of the person she thought was inside.

She raised her hand to gently tap at the door and…

Suddenly, Laura felt the door slipping away from her. She was moving backwards, falling, no, being pulled. Someone was pulling her.

"I told you to stay away," Melanie's hand was tugging at her hair, dragging her.

Laura shrieked as Melanie yanked her along the landing.

"Carley!" she just about managed to say before Melanie slapped her hand over Laura's mouth.

"Stop that noise. We do have neighbours. We run a tight house here. A quiet house. You keep your voice down."

Laura had little choice as Melanie's hand gripped tightly across her mouth.

As Melanie pulled Laura into the large bedroom, Laura heard a noise like some kind of animal scratching in the room she had almost entered.

"Mmmmfh," was the closest Laura could get to a word.

"Hush now," Melanie said. "I'm going to take my hand off your mouth and you're going to keep very quiet or something bad is going to happen."

Laura's mind was whirring. Should she try to bite Melanie? Kick out at her? Her eyes darted around the room; looking for something, anything that she might be able to use.

Use for what, though? She was an estate agent from Sheffield, not Jack Reacher. The extent of her survival skills was the two years she had spent as a girl guide, learning how to tie knots and build a fire. That wasn't going to help her now.

The room was painfully tidy, almost clinically clean. Laura tried to take in as much detail as she could before Melanie tugged on her mouth, lifting her face up to look at her instead.

"Do you understand me? Because I have to say, Laura, you don't seem to have understood much about what I've said to you so far."

Laura locked eyes with Melanie and gave her a nod. Whatever the bad thing was that would happen if she screamed again, she didn't want any of it.

Melanie moved her hand back, just slightly at first, as though testing to see whether Laura would keep to her wordless word. When Laura did indeed remain silent, she withdrew and took a step away.

"Good," she said. "Okay. Now listen, your friend Charley has promised to be a quiet, good girl too, but somehow, I didn't trust her as much as I trust you. There's something about her that I find inherently untrustworthy."

"What have…" Laura spoke quietly, but Melanie reached forward and placed two fingers firmly onto her lips.

"Being quiet means not asking questions," Melanie said.

"Okay," Laura mumbled. "Okay."

"She's fine. Just having a little nap."

No matter how much Laura wanted to yell out, she realised she had to bide her time, play along for the present.

Melanie lifted a chair over from in front of the smart Scandinavian style dresser. She didn't drag it across the floor as Laura would have, but instead raised it and carried it to rest in front of her.

"Let's have a talk, Laura. Face to face. Woman to woman."

Laura looked at her without speaking. She didn't want to make Melanie any angrier that she already was. The thought of Carley downstairs and the fear of what might have happened to her was overwhelming.

Laura could feel her heart skittering in her chest like an insect trying to escape from a sealed container.

"First. Give me your phone."

Laura's phone was her lifeline. Her connection to her mother, and now, her connection to any kind of help she might be able to get. She was in no position to argue with Melanie, though, so she dug into her pocket and handed over the phone.

"Thank you," Melanie said. "You won't be needing that for a while. I'll tell you want though, just so you know it's safe, I'm going to lock it away for you. Okay?"

Again, Laura couldn't really disagree, so she watched as Melanie opened a small safe at the top of her wardrobe and slid Laura's prized possession inside. Then, Melanie sat back down across from Laura and began to talk.

"You're a reasonable woman, aren't you? Of course you are. You thought you were doing something good, coming here, coming all this way to help… well, you didn't even know who you were coming to help, did you? How very noble of you. What a dear, sweet heart you must have to put yourself in danger to help a stranger. Stranger danger." Melanie gave a slight chuckle. "And now look."

"What have you done to Carley?" Laura spoke quietly and calmly, trying her best to moderate her tone so as not to upset Melanie. "And what are you going to do to me?"

Melanie put her fingers to her own lips this time.

"Gerrard is on his way, and he's going to help me sort all of this out when he comes home. Until then, let's talk. And by let's talk, I mean I'll talk and you can listen to me. You will listen to me."

It didn't appear Laura had any option than to do exactly what Melanie told her.

Be Safe.

She heard Catharine's voice floating around her head. She wished she were back at home with her mum now, that she had never found the note, or set out on this stupid, dangerous adventure. Now she was stuck in a strange room with an unpredictable woman, and she did not know how she was going to get out of the mess she had created for herself.

CHAPTER TWENTY-NINE

Melanie was so unnaturally relaxed that it unsettled Laura even further than it would have if the woman were yelling at her.

"I never wanted any of this," Melanie spoke calmly, as though they were two regular women having an everyday chat over a coffee, rather than two strangers, captor and captive.

"This wasn't how we planned things," Melanie continued. "You have to believe that. Neither of us wanted to hurt her."

Laura's expression slipped slightly, her eyebrows lifting, and her eyes widening just enough so that Melanie noticed her reaction.

"Not physically. Whatever you think is going on here, you have to know that we have never hurt her. Not like that. We aren't bad people, Laura. I know you think we are some kind of sociopathic monsters, but we are normal people that just wanted a better life."

Without knowing exactly what Melanie was talking about, it was difficult for Laura to add to the jigsaw puzzle that she had already been finding impossible to piece together. It wasn't clear to her whether her captor thought she knew more than she did, or whether Melanie had an overwhelming need to talk about what was happening without bothering to fill in the assumed detail. Either way, very little was making sense.

"I can't let you open that door, I'm afraid, Laura."

Melanie leaned forwards in almost an identical way to how Gerrard had swept in towards her the previous day. The two of them were the same in so many ways. Her breath was fresh though, and far less distasteful than her husband's, even though her proximity made Laura's skin bristle.

"Gerry and I have done so much to make sure that nothing endangers what we have here. It wasn't easy for us. It wasn't easy for him, at first, accepting what we had to do, but…"

Laura shook her head. "You are monsters. You can't just keep someone locked away in a room."

"Locked away?" Melanie let a sharp laugh ring from her plummy lips. "If you had tried that door handle, you'd have known that it isn't locked. No one is locked away. All you had to do was walk up to the door and push it open. But I'll tell you what I told her. If you open that door, you are never leaving this house."

"Her?" Laura picked up on the word.

Melanie tilted her head to the side.

"You're a clever one, aren't you, Laura? The most colourful crayon in the box, I'm sure. You spend your time reading those oh so clever books. Mysteries and murders everywhere. How lovely it would be for you to be able to brighten up your dreary little life by getting involved in a real-life mystery of your own. The detective saves the day, and they all live happily ever after."

Melanie moved so close to Laura that she could almost brush lips with her. It was a bizarre, irregular thought to have, but Laura had never been that close to anyone without it leading to a kiss. The whole situation was surreal, and Laura's brain was clearly struggling to make sense of it.

"Not this time, Laura," Melanie said. "You're not going to save anyone. Nobody needs to be saved. Everything is running along quite perfectly here, and you are going to back the hell down and let us get on with our lives."

Laura didn't back down. Instead, she repeated the same word that she had said to Melanie. "Her?"

Melanie pushed Laura backwards, so that she fell flat onto the bed. It didn't hurt, apart from where Melanie's bony fingertips had pressed into her breastbone.

Sprawled on the bed, Laura looked across at Melanie, who sitting at eye-level to her.

"Go home, Laura. I'm giving you one last chance to go home and forget about all of this. You're at a fork in the road here. One way, you leave this house and you and your friend get into her crappy little car and go back to your crappy little lives."

Laura couldn't help but think of what Gerrard had said the previous day. He had referred to her *little life,* too. What was so bad about her life, though? Times had been unbearably difficult recently, that was true, but neither Gerrard nor Melanie knew anything about that. They were judging her based upon what she had told them and the image that she had projected – the image of the person she was before her life had started to fall apart. Still, they had both talked about her life as if it was somehow lacking. Even in the state that she had been living for the past four months, she couldn't bear to hear their disdain for her day-to-day existence. She had a good job. She had her mum. She had friends. She had spent the last four months locked deep inside her own misery, but those things, those good, good things, were real, and they were anything but little.

"What's the other way?" Laura asked, fixing Melanie with a stony stare, which she hoped looked more fearless than she felt.

Melanie laughed again.

"I touched a nerve, didn't I? Look around you, Laura. Look at everything that we have, Gerrard and I. This is what a good life looks like. This is how you could live, one day, if you weren't such a mouse. Isn't this the kind of life that you aspire to?"

"With all respect, Melanie, you know nothing about my life."

Laura tried to remain calm. She needed to keep her wits about her and her emotions in check. What Melanie was saying was adding fuel to the fire that was already burning within her. The woman had done something to Carley, and had done other things to whoever was in the next room. Laura didn't know what any of those things were, but now the woman was doing things to her and was capable of plenty more.

"I know that you're here chasing stories, trying to get some excitement into your boring life, my dear. We have done too much to get *this* life to let you get in the way. Neither of us is going to let you ruin this for us. So the other way, if you aren't prepared to leave and let us live our happy lives in peace, well, it isn't going to work out well for you."

Laura watched Melanie's expression as she spoke. Despite the words that were coming from her mouth, Melanie was not actually saying what she was threatening to do. She hadn't said that she would hurt Laura or detain her there. Whilst the threat had been made, Melanie didn't seem willing to state what her threat actually was.

"I can't walk away," Laura said, as calmly as she could manage. She pushed her hands into the bed and tried to bring herself up to a sitting position again. Melanie watched, not helping, but not stopping her.

"Then what, exactly, do you plan to do?" Melanie asked.

Laura looked Melanie in the eyes, and with one more push, she launched herself at the woman. Although Melanie was taller than her, she was sitting, and as Laura flew towards her, her weight toppled Melanie onto the floor.

"See what happens," Laura said, much more calmly than the situation should have elicited.

She stood over Melanie, unsure of what to do next, letting her instincts guide her.

Melanie reached out for Laura's leg, tugging at her, trying to bring her to the floor.

The room was so insanely tidy that there was nothing she could use as a defensive weapon. As Melanie tightened her grip on Laura's leg, Laura's reflexes kicked in. She grabbed the object that was closest to her and launched it at the scrabbling woman.

Unfortunately for Melanie, the closest object was the chair that Laura had toppled her from.

Melanie let out a sickening grunt as the back of the chair made contact with her face, striking her full-on with a force that Laura was sure could have broken her nose. And then, she was still and silent.

A stream of curse words ran through Laura's mind as she looked down at the unmoving body in front of her. Although knocking Melanie out was certainly not the worst thing she could have done, Laura had never physically hurt anyone before, and it felt so far out of character that she wasn't quite sure how to respond.

"Do what you came for," she told herself.

She gave the numbers on the safe a quick press to see if she could open it and retrieve her phone, but it was hopeless without the code.

All she had to do was to decide whether to go down to check on Carley first, or to finally find out who was in the room next door. Laura made a split-second decision and stepped over Melanie, heading out of the room and onto the landing.

CHAPTER THIRTY

Laura pushed open the door and finally saw exactly who she needed to help. Everything became clear at that moment. All the scrambled puzzle pieces snapped into position, and the big picture revealed itself.

There, sitting on the edge of the bed, was a woman. She didn't even turn her eyes towards the door when Laura walked in. Instead, she continued doing exactly what she had been doing: reading a book.

"I'm not hungry," she said, her voice cracked and dry, like a riverbed that hadn't seen water for a long barren season.

"Hello?" Laura said, trying to keep her nerves in check, and also not wanting to scare the woman on the bed.

Whatever Laura had expected, it was not this. The woman was most definitely not Melanie and Gerrard's daughter. Her hair was pinned up at the back, with wisps falling around the sides of her face, but it was a dark grey. She had probably once had deep chocolate-coloured curls, but now they were the shade of ashes.

She was wearing a simple long plain navy dress, not a nightdress, as someone who was bedridden might wear, but a regular smart-looking frock. Were it not for the fact that Laura suspected that the woman had been kept in this room for quite some time, she would have thought that she was simply spending some time alone in her bedroom, reading, much as Laura liked to do herself.

The woman finally turned at the sound of Laura's voice. Her expression changed in a flash. She had been calm when Laura arrived, lost in her own world. As soon as she saw Laura, she snapped her book closed and shuffled quickly up the bed away from her.

"Go!" she said, her voice crackling. "Go, now."

Laura reached out one hand, moving slowly, as if approaching a wounded animal.

"It's okay," she said. "I'm Laura. I got your note. I'm here to help you."

The woman in the bed looked at Laura, reading her face as though it were a book.

"Laura?" she said, eventually.

“That’s right,” she replied, bobbing her head slightly. “I found your note,” Laura repeated. “Come with me. I’ve come to get you out of here.”

“Out.” The woman echoed the word but made no move to join Laura. Instead, she pulled her legs up towards her, wrapping her arms around them and hugging herself in a tight ball.

“It’s alright,” Laura said. She felt the urgency of getting the woman out of the bed, out of the room and out of the house before Melanie woke, and especially before Gerrard returned home. She felt that urgency, but she tried to keep it under control. The last thing she wanted was for the woman to panic. She needed her to trust her, and she needed it to happen fast.

Laura looked at the book that the woman had dropped onto the bed when she withdrew. It was one that she recognised.

“That’s a good book,” Laura said, pointing at the cover. “What do you think of it?”

The woman looked at the book and then looked back at Laura, but did not reply.

"How far are you into it? There's a fantastic bit, near the beginning. When the friend first disappears…"

"It's a good book," the woman in the bed said, almost echoing Laura's words.

"It is," Laura replied. "I have lots of books that you can borrow," she said, clutching at straws, trying to find any way to get the woman to connect with her.

"Melanie brings me books," she said. "Gerry didn't want her to, but Melanie looks after me."

She raised her hand to her mouth as though she had said too much and wanted to stop herself from saying anything else.

"It's all right," Laura said. "Melanie can't hear us. You can talk."

The last thing she wanted was to spend any more time in the room than was necessary, but something told Laura that taking a few minutes to reassure the woman was going to be worthwhile. She gestured towards the end of the bed in an unspoken question, and then sat perched on the edge.

"What's your name?" Laura asked.

"Jean," the woman replied. She continued to watch Laura cautiously, like a garden bird might observe a cat stalking at the other end of the yard.

"Hello Jean," Laura said. "Listen, I want to help you. I read your note, and my friend and I have come here to help you."

When Jean looked puzzled, Laura spoke again.

"You left a note in a book. Melanie or Gerrard took that book to a charity shop, and my friend bought that book. Then, well, she sent it to me. I got your note."

"Melanie's note," Jean smiled in apparent recognition.

"Melanie's?" Laura felt the puzzle pieces starting to scatter, as though someone had upended the table on which she had been building the jigsaw. "Melanie's note?"

"I wrote it for her. I thought she would find it when she read the book. She always reads my books when I've finished with them, and then we talk about them afterwards." Jean was actually smiling fondly, whilst Laura was frowning, trying to make sense of what Jean was saying.

"You wanted Melanie to help you? But…" Laura looked around her. "Isn't it Melanie that keeps you here?"

Jean gasped in a way that would have seemed melodramatic if it weren't for the circumstances. "Not Melanie! Melanie looks after me. Melanie brings me food and books and clothes and…" She shook her head constantly as she spoke. "Without Melanie…" She stopped, as though she couldn't bring herself to imagine what would happen without the woman that was lying unconscious on the floor in the next room.

None of it made sense.

Laura thought of the only question that she could ask that might help.

"Why do you need help, Jean?"

Jean looked over Laura's shoulder, over to the open door and beyond. A chill of panic rippled through Laura, and she span to see whether there was someone standing there. Had Melanie come round already, or worse still, was it Gerrard?

As she thought the word, Jean let out a low hissing noise.

"My son," she said, as though the word was painful for her to speak. "Gerry."

CHAPTER THIRTY-ONE

If it wasn't Melanie that she needed help from, then of course it had to be Gerrard. What surprised Laura, though, was that Jean saw Melanie as her saviour, rather than as Gerrard's co-conspirator. She realised, after her confrontation with Melanie in the bedroom, that whatever Gerrard was doing, Melanie was complicit in. Melanie might have been the one that fed and cared for Jean, but she was still part of the problem. She was still keeping Jean here in this room. Wasn't she?

Laura had to check her assumption.

"When was the last time you went outside?" she asked.

Jean shook her head. "He doesn't let me out. And she… Melanie says it's too dangerous. He would find out and punish us both. I can't let that happen to her after all she does for me. One night, I needed the toilet when they were both asleep. I couldn't wait. I'm not meant to leave the room without them, but I couldn't wait. I couldn't." A single tear ran down Jean's cheek. "He woke up. I tried to be as quiet as I could, I really did, and I would have gone straight back to my room, but he… he woke up." Streams flooded down her cheeks.

"I'm sorry, Jean," Laura said. She wanted to ask what had happened, what he had done, but she didn't want to hear the answer.

"I have to stay in my room."

"Not anymore," Laura said. "I've come to help you. You don't have to stay here anymore."

"You have to take Melanie too," Jean said. "You can't leave her here with him."

As badly as Laura wanted to tell Jean that Melanie was just as evil as her husband, Jean's son, she bit her lip and said nothing.

"I'll come back for her," she lied. "I need to get you out before Gerrard comes home."

"Thursday afternoon. One o'clock." Jean spoke as though she was reading out a calendar appointment.

"What?" Laura said.

"Thursday afternoon. One o'clock."

What time was it now? Her phone was locked away in Melanie and Gerrard's bedroom, and she had never seen the need to have a watch. She tried to think back over the events of the morning. They had set off from the hotel at almost eleven, got here at twenty past. There was all the fuss getting into the house, and then she must have spent at least half an hour with Melanie. If it wasn't already one, it was getting close.

"He gets home at one o'clock?" Laura asked, with urgency.

"Thursday afternoon…" Jean said again.

"Yes, yes," Laura said. "I get it."

She jumped up and stepped towards Jean. She had tried to be as patient and peaceful as she could, but time appeared to be running out. They had to get downstairs, get Carley, and get out.

Carley. In all the commotion, she hadn't exactly forgotten about Carley, but she had been focussed on her own situation and what she was doing upstairs. What had happened downstairs was a different dilemma. Carley hadn't come up to find her, or to help her, so Laura could only assume that she was still incapacitated. Should she leave Jean here, run down and check on Carley and then come back for the old woman? There was no time. They had to move, and quickly.

Laura reached out her hand towards Jean, but the woman didn't put her own hand out to grab it. Laura looked her in the eye for a moment, before bending to pick up the book.

"Let's take it with us," she said.

Jean nodded once, slowly.

"You need to finish it so you can talk to Melanie about it," Laura said, trying to smile, even though she felt anything but positive.

Jean held her hand towards Laura and took the book from her. With her other hand, she grasped hold of Laura. Laura awkwardly pulled Jean up off the bed and onto her feet.

For someone who had spent however long she had in this room, Jean was surprisingly steady on her feet. Laura wrapped her arm around her still though and guided the woman towards the door.

As they reached the threshold between bedroom and landing, Jean stopped dead in her tracks.

For a heart-stopping moment, Laura thought she had left the Wexlers' bedroom door open, and that Jean had seen her daughter-in-law lying there on the floor. Her eyes darted across the landing, and she felt a flood of relief when she saw it was closed.

Still, Jean stood, not moving.

"It's okay," Laura said. "He's not here. I'm going to take you somewhere that he can't hurt you."

Jean studied Laura's face, and Laura hoped she couldn't read her nerves and the desperate fear that they were going to get caught if they didn't hurry.

As they stepped forward, onto the landing, Jean let out a long breath. It was almost as though she had been holding it in the entire time she had been in the bedroom. Laura did not know how long that could possibly be and couldn't let her mind start to speculate about that now. They had to get moving. They had to get Carley. They had to get out.

CHAPTER THIRTY-TWO

Laura helped Jean down the stairs, not because being in the room had disabled her in any way, but because the woman was old, and not as nimble as she herself was. How old exactly, Laura hadn't worked out. Gerrard and Melanie looked to be in their forties, so Jean was probably at least late sixties, or more likely her seventies. Older than her own mother, Catharine, that was for certain.

As they stepped quickly but carefully down the stairs, Laura had a deep, invasive thought. How could someone treat their mother like this? Her mother meant everything to her and had literally been everything to her over the past four months. Without Catharine, she would have struggled beyond belief. And here, all this time, Gerrard had been keeping his own mother under house arrest. Why? What good was it to anybody?

When they reached the bottom of the stairs, they could finally see Carley.

"Oh my!" Jean exclaimed.

"Carley!"

Laura ran over to where Carley was sitting, slumped against the wall.

"Hey, Carley! Are you all right? Carley? Can you hear me?"

Laura crouched beside her friend and gently patted her cheek. She had never had to rouse anyone like this before. Was she meant to slap Carley or try to wake her more softly than that?

"Carley!" she repeated.

Carley groaned quietly and opened her eyes.

"Grrr," she mumbled.

"Shh," Laura urged. "Don't try to talk. We've got to get out of here."

"Grrr," Carley moaned again, more loudly.

Laura reached to pull her up to her feet.

"Grrr!" Carley pointed at something behind Laura, and Laura finally twigged.

Gerrard was standing in the doorframe, looking at the three women. One clambering to her feet, one standing sheepishly against the wall, and the other now looking straight at him.

"Ladies," he said, with the same false charm that he had used on them the previous day. He gazed at each of them in turn, finally letting his eyes settle on Jean.

"Mum," he said, his voice filled with feigned disappointment. "What are you doing down here?" He looked down at her hand. "I'm not interrupting your book club, am I?"

"Gerry, please. I'm sorry. I was…"

"No," Laura said, firmly. "Don't, Jean."

She stepped in front of the old woman protectively.

"How sweet," Gerrard said. "How very sweet." He stared at his mother with the kind of look that could freeze hot tea. "You're going to regret this, Mummy," he said.

Laura could feel the woman trembling next to her.

"It's you that's going to regret it," she said.

Her words sounded like they were being spoken by someone else. She was so far from her usual sheepish shyness that it felt like someone had inhabited her body and was driving her forwards.

Without even thinking about what to do, Laura reached out to Jean and the novel that she was gripping as though her life depended on it.

"Sorry," Laura whispered. "You'll get it back."

Laura grabbed the book and flung it for everything she was worth at Gerrard, aiming for his face.

The corner of the spine made contact with Gerard's eye, and he staggered backwards, his hand clutching his face.

"You…"

But Laura didn't wait to hear what insult he was about to hurl at her. Instead, she reached behind, grasping for Jean's hand.

"Carley," she shouted, "Let's go!"

Carley wasted no time in wobbling to her feet and heading for the door. She darted past Gerrard and hurried to the exit.

Jean gave Gerrard one lingering look before allowing Laura to lead her along behind Carley.

"Jean Wexler, you come back here right now."

He didn't even call her 'Mum', Laura thought as they reached the door.

Carley pulled at the doorknob, but nothing happened.

"Locked!" she yelped, moving her hand to flick down the switch and open the Yale lock. There was a bolt across the top of the door, and she stretched up to fumble it across.

Laura moved Jean in front of her, between the two of them. Looking back over her shoulder, she saw Gerrard getting to his feet. It wouldn't be long before he was up and coming for them.

"Quick!" Laura urged. "He's coming."

She didn't want to cause Carley to panic and make a mistake with the lock, and she definitely didn't want to scare Jean, but the urgency was clear.

"I'm trying," Carley said, giving the bolt a last tug that released it and allowed her to pull the door open.

Cold air rushed into the house, and Jean lifted her face into it.

"Come on," Carley said, guiding Jean out of the door and onto the path.

And then two things happened at once.

Behind them, Gerrard reached out and grabbed Laura, pulling her back with such force that the pair of them tumbled in a heap onto the parquet floor. It was hard, and Laura's hip collided with the wood with a sharp thud.

Meanwhile, Carley and Jean were stopped dead in their tracks. As they rushed along the path. They were brought to a standstill by a figure at the gate. Someone lifted the latch and stood just inside the garden, looking at them. He didn't speak, he didn't move; he stared at the two women.

"Oh man," Carley said, beneath her breath. "What now?"

She stepped in front of Jean, ready for another confrontation.

In the hallway, Laura was on her back, on top of Gerrard. She rubbed at her hip and then cycled her limbs, like a beetle trying to right itself. The speed with which he had come behind her, grabbed her, and the two of them had hit the floor had not given her time to think about what was happening. However, as she pressed her palms to the cold wooden floor and lifted herself up, she realised that there was nothing, or rather nobody, holding her back. Gerrard wasn't trying to stop her. In fact, he wasn't doing anything at all. He was limp and motionless, and as Laura got to her feet and looked down at him, she understood why.

Whilst her fall had been almost completely cushioned by the presence of Gerard's body – all apart from her hip – he had not been so lucky. Nothing had been behind him or beneath him when he fell but the heavy wood of the banister. His head had made contact with the polished oak and was now a couple of inches to the side of it, a pool of dark blood forming like a halo.

"Oh, my…" Laura felt a combination of panic and nausea, the overwhelming mix making her head swim.

No matter how she felt about the man who was lying beside her, Laura was taken aback by the sight, and by her own actions.

She nudged Gerard's body with her foot. It felt like pressing against a sandbag, firm and heavy. He gave no response.

"Carley!" Laura tried to yell, but no sound came out of her mouth. She cleared her throat and tried again. "Carley!"

Laura had to force herself to turn her eyes away from Gerrard and the growing deep crimson pool in which he lay. When she did, she saw through the door and into the garden beyond and was stunned to see Carley and Jean standing on the path.

She already had a gut feeling that something was wrong. They should have run straight to the car. Neither of them was turning to look behind them to see where she was. They were… what *were* they doing?

Laura stumbled forwards, rubbing her hip as she moved. It was throbbing, but the pain was only slowing her. It didn't feel as though she had done any serious damage to herself in the fall.

There was someone else in the garden. She couldn't see who from her focal point in the hallway, but she was sure that's what had stopped them. The way they were standing, almost clustered, was a giveaway. A delivery person, perhaps? A neighbour who had heard the commotion?

Laura kept her distance, watching from the hallway until she could be sure of what was happening. The last thing she wanted to do was to walk into more trouble.

What she saw surprised her almost as much as everything else that had happened so far that day. Laura stood only a few feet from Gerard's unconscious body and looked up to see Jamie.

Her husband was standing in the doorframe, staring at the scene inside the hallway.

It was a full twenty seconds before Jamie spoke.

"What the hell happened here?" he said.

"What are you *doing* here?" Laura gasped. "Mum sent you?"

"She didn't send me. She was worried about you. She told me where you were, and then I was worried about you too."

He looked down at the man sprawled on the floor.

"It looks like I didn't need to be."

Laura shook her head. "Everything is under control," she said. It wasn't exactly the truth, but her pumping adrenaline was giving her the same kind of confidence that her smart work suits and slick make-up used to.

Carley had her arm around Jean, guiding her onward down the path, towards the car.

"I met your new friends?" Jamie said, gesturing to Carley and the old woman. "Seems like they got off lightly compared to…" He looked down at Gerrard. "Laura. Is he dead?"

"Look, we need to get out of here before Gerrard and his wife upstairs get back on their feet, so if you wouldn't mind please moving out of the way…?"

Jamie's face was a picture of astonished surprise.

"His wife? How many people have you…?" Jamie bent over and pressed two fingers against the pulse point on Gerrard's neck. "Okay, he's not dead. That's something. What about the other one? Where is she? What have you done, Laura?"

"Well, it's a long story," Laura said. "Really, we've got to go." She wanted to know why he was in Cambridge and what he was hoping to achieve by being there, but there was no time to quibble about the details.

Laura assumed that her husband's dumbstruck expression was not just down to the unconscious, bleeding man on the floor, but also because he'd never seen Laura like this before, or at least not for a long time.

"I'll explain everything," she urged, "but please, let's go."

"Should I phone the police? Have you called them?"

"Jamie, my phone is upstairs, locked away in the safe, in a bedroom where I hit this man's wife over the head with a chair. Yes, she's alive too, before you ask. But I'm not going up there. Not now and not ever. When we get out of here, and I stress again that we should be getting out of here, I'll tell you everything and we can phone the police. But for now," she said, her voice getting louder as she spoke, "Let's go!"

She looked down at Gerrard one more time and shuddered. Then she stepped forward, past Jamie, and strode purposefully down the path to Carley's car.

Jamie hurried behind her, calling out to her as she ran.

"Where shall I meet you?" he shouted.

"Shh!" Laura waved her hands, parting the air in front of her. She paused, just before she got into the car and bustled back over to where Jamie was standing in the middle of the street.

"Don't make a scene," she said. "If we can get back to our hotel, we can sort everything out from there, okay? We're staying at the Sunshine Hotel. Meet us there."

And with that, Laura climbed into the passenger seat of Carley's car, turned to talk to Jean, comfortable in the back, and didn't even look to see Jamie watching them as they drove off.

CHAPTER THIRTY-THREE

Back at the hotel, the four of them crammed into the small room. It was time to phone the police and let them know what had happened.

Carley settled Jean onto the bed with a strong, sweet mug of tea whilst Laura made the call.

"They're on their way," she said, handing Jamie's phone back to him. "Hopefully, they'll be able to recover my phone for me."

"On their way here or there?"

Laura paused and looked confused.

"I didn't ask them to specify. Uh, both, maybe? They said someone would be with us soon, anyway."

"Do you want to let your mum know you're all right?" Jamie said, waving his phone back towards Laura.

She looked at Jean, and then back at Jamie. "How could anyone do this to their mother?" she asked, reaching out to take him up on the offer.

"Beats me," Carley said. "I'm just glad we've got you here, Jean."

Jean sipped at her tea and kept her eyes down-turned, lost in her own thoughts.

"But why?" Jamie asked. "Why would your son do that? Why would he keep you in that room? I don't understand."

Jean shook her head, the sadness in her eyes saying more than she could.

Finally, she spoke. "I don't know," she said. "When his father died, I said that he and Mel could move into the house. She's such a lovely woman. You must let her know where I am. She'll be terribly worried."

Laura shot a quick glance towards Carley and Carley shook her head.

"And then… what? They just locked you in there?" Jamie wouldn't stop with the questions.

"There's going to be enough of that when the police get here," Laura admonished him. "Leave it for now. It doesn't matter why, all that matters is that we've got her out of there. The police will sort everything out from here."

"They would probably have sorted it all out in the first place if you…"

Laura cut off Jamie's words with a sharp look.

"Do you not think we went to them first? They were hopeless. That's why the two of us are here. We did what anyone would. We found Jean, and we got her out."

The conversation was getting them nowhere, and Laura was relieved when the room's phone rang.

"Ms Jacobs, there are some visitors here for you," the receptionist said. "Two police officers."

"Send them up," Laura said. She had already decided that it would be better for Jean to talk to them in the comfort of the hotel room rather than having to sit in the lobby with all kinds of passers-by listening in to the details of her life.

When she had put the phone down, she turned to Jean. "Everything is going to be all right now," she said. "We're going to make sure that everything is going to be all right."

The two officers that arrived at the room were a tall, slim woman and a shorter, squat man. Their faces were friendly, but serious. They meant business, which was far preferable to the demeanour of the dismissive officer that had spoken to Laura on the telephone days earlier.

"Come in," she said, showing them through to the room.

It was already cramped with Jean and Carley sitting on the bed and Jamie perched on the little table next to the kettle. The officers squeezed in and stood with their backs against the wall.

"I understand you've had quite an exciting day," the female officer said, to no one in particular and everyone in general.

"I'm officer Cartwright, and this is Baker."

"Harry," the male police officer said with a smile.

"Why don't you tell me what's happened?"

Carley and Laura exchanged another look, and Carley nodded in Laura's direction.

"You can tell them," she said.

And so again, Laura retold the entire series of events, from the time she received the book and found the note, the backstory of how Carley had come to own the book in the first place, and their journey to Cambridge.

When it came to telling them about how she had escaped from Melanie, she paused.

"Jean is very fond of her daughter-in-law," she said. "But I'm afraid she might not be as nice a person as Jean believes. Melanie…" she sighed and looked at Jean. "Melanie was just as much a part of this as her husband. I'm sorry, Jean."

"She looked after me…" Jean insisted.

Cartwright scribbled something on her pad and nodded for Laura to continue.

"Melanie threatened me and then she… she tried to hold me captive in her bedroom. I had to escape, and so…" Laura swallowed heavily and had to break eye contact with Jean as she continued. "I'm afraid I hit her. I knocked her off the chair and then I hit her. With the chair."

Cartwright stared at Laura, and Laura looked between her and Baker.

"It was self-defence, of course," she said. "She had already told me what had happened to Carley…"

"And you were, at this time, unconscious in the kitchen?" Cartwright directed the question at Carley.

"Yes," she said. "She's right, Melanie is dangerous. She attacked me. Hit me on the head with a coffee maker, of all things."

Laura's eyes widened at that. She had known the general outline of what had happened, but not this detail.

"A coffee maker?" Baker asked, as though not believing what he was hearing.

"You know, like a Gaggia. One of those machines you can get to make latte and stuff."

"Latte and stuff," Cartwright said, writing in her notebook. "I know what a coffee maker is. Ignore this Luddite. Okay, carry on, Laura. You hit Melanie Wexler with a chair and…?"

"And she, er, became unconscious."

Laura looked over at Jamie, who was watching her in silence. What must he think of her? He was probably happy that he had got away from her. All of this could only confirm his decision to leave her. Instead of frowning or shaking his head, though, he smiled kindly.

"It's okay," he said. "Go on, Laura."

Laura dug deep and found the courage to continue recalling the events.

"I ran into the other room and found Jean. We went downstairs, and that's when I saw Gerrard."

Laura screwed her eyes up tightly closed as the image of Gerrard, lying on the floor in the pool of blood, exploded into her mind.

"And you had the altercation that led to you also knocking *him* out?" Cartwright raised an eyebrow as she asked Laura the question.

"You have to believe that this isn't something that I go around doing regularly," she said.

"I can vouch for that," Jamie finally spoke. "Laura is my wife, and she's the most gentle, laid-back person I know."

My wife. Not my ex-wife or my future ex-wife. My wife.

"Thank you, Mr, er, Jacobs," Cartwright said.

"She wouldn't have done it unless she had to," Carley agreed.

"We've sent officers to the scene," Cartwright said. "Mr Wexler, your son,

Mrs Wexler, is in a bad way, I'm afraid. But he is stable, for now. Melanie was already up on her feet when the officers arrived, but the two of them have been taken to hospital, anyway. Always best with possible head injuries,"

"Are the officers still with them? You can't let them get away with this..." Laura said urgently.

Cartwright held up a hand.

"There are officers at the hospital, and when Mr and Mrs Wexler are in a fit condition, you can be certain we will be speaking to them, to hear their side of this." Cartwright turned to Jean. "Mrs Wexler, I know this must be very difficult for you, but can you confirm what Ms Jacobs here has said?"

"Melanie is a lovely woman," Jean said.

Laura looked at her with frustration bubbling in her veins.

"But you *were* forced to stay in that room?" Cartwright asked.

Jean nodded.

"By both your son and Melanie?"

Jean nodded again, but said, "She only made me stay so that he didn't get angry with us. He would have punished both of us if she…"

"But she never let you out either? Even when you were alone together?"

"No," Jean said, quietly.

"And did they ever hurt you? Physically? Did they actually ever *punish* you?"

"No," Jean said.

"Does that matter?" Carley butted in. "She was a prisoner. Isn't that bad enough?"

"Wait," Baker said, motioning for her to be quiet.

"No," Jean said again. "Never. Neither of them."

"What about the bills for the house?"

Cartwright seemed to change direction suddenly.

"Bills?" Jean asked.

"Who paid for the food, gas, electricity? You owned the house, did you?"

"Oh, I don't know," Jean said. "I owned it, yes. Well, my husband Charles and I did until he died. Then Mel and Gerry moved in with me, to look after me. Gerry… well, he took it too far, I suppose.

It started off with him keeping me in the house, and then he didn't want me to leave the room."

"Did you write a note? The note that Laura said she found in a book?"

Jean turned her eyes down to the floor and then looked back up at Cartwright. She nodded once, slowly.

"I wanted to get out," she said. "I haven't been in the sunshine for so long. Gerry was… he keeps getting annoyed at me. Everything I do makes him angry, so angry, and I… I thought if I asked Melanie, she would help me."

"You couldn't ask her when she went in the room to check on you?"

"I tried," Jean said. Her eyes were wide and red, and Laura could see the tears that were about to spill out.

"You had had enough?" Laura asked.

"Ms Jacobs," Baker said. "Let Mrs Wexler speak, please."

Jean let out a long, pained sigh. "He wanted to move me into a home," she said. "Melanie wouldn't let him. And I don't want it. I don't want to go. I just want to be free to live in my house with Mel and Gerry. He said that I could stay but that I have to stay in the room. If I tried to get out again, he said he would have me put in a home. I can't… I don't want that." She was crying uncontrollably now, and Laura reached onto the counter to pass her a tissue.

"It's okay," she said. "It's okay."

Whatever Gerrard and Melanie had been doing, the psychological torment of the threat of moving Jean into a care home was unbelievably cruel.

"Okay," Cartwright said, snapping her book closed. "I think we have all we need for now. We will have you all in to make statements and take it from there. How long are you staying in Cambridge, Ms Jacobs? Ms Brooks?"

"We were meant to go home today," Carley said. "But we'll be going home tomorrow."

Cartwright shook her head. "Add another day onto your visit and come in to see us tomorrow." She handed a card to Laura. "The station isn't far from here."

"What about Jean?" Laura asked. "Where will she go?"

"Do you want to go home, Jean?" Baker asked.

Jean shook her head. “No,” she said.

“You’d let her go back there?” Jamie barked. “After everything that’s happened?”

“Officer Baker asked whether she wanted to. Nobody said that we would send her back there. You can come with us, Mrs Wexler, and we can find somewhere for you to stay whilst everything is sorted out, or…” Cartwright looked at Carley and Laura. “You can stay with these ladies.”

There was no space in the hotel room for an extra person, let alone two, if Jamie were to stay. It didn’t matter.

“Of course she can,” Laura said. “Jean, we would be happy for you to stay here with us, if that’s what you want.”

“I’m not going to go into a home,” she said. “That’s what Gerry wants; that’s what the police want.”

“We would find somewhere suitable…” Cartwright responded, but Jean shook her head.

“No,” she said resolutely. “If these kind girls don’t mind, I’m going to stay with them.”

Cartwright looked between the women again and gave them a nod.

"But please, let me know how Melanie is. I'm worried about her."

"We have Mr Jacobs's number," Cartwright said. "And we'll try to get your phone back to the station so you can collect it tomorrow, Mrs Jacobs.

Laura smiled. "Thank you," she said. It was strange not having her phone with her, but mainly she wanted to talk to her mum. She knew she couldn't keep texting on Jamie's phone, and she felt lost without her own device.

The police officers left as abruptly as they had arrived, and the four of them were left in the room, struggling to take in what had happened.

CHAPTER THIRTY-FOUR

There was no way that the four people would fit into the hotel room that Carley and Laura had been staying in. They had to stay the extra night so that they could visit the police station in the morning, but they hadn't thought through the practicalities.

"I'll book another room," Jamie said. "You and I can share, and Jean can stay here with Carley. That makes the most sense."

Laura swallowed hard. She had spent her first weeks away from Jamie wishing that they could be together, and then the following three months trying to avoid even talking to him. Sharing a room with him seemed like the ultimate in awkwardness. If she refused, though, it would only make her look immature.

"Okay," Laura said. She didn't know whether to be clear that he should book a twin room, but again, didn't want to say or do anything that would reveal her anxiety over the situation. There was enough to worry about without causing a scene with her ex-husband.

When Jamie went down to the lobby to make the arrangements, Carley finally had a chance to talk to her friend.

"Are you okay?" she asked. It was a ridiculous question. There was nothing to be okay about.

"Yes," Laura said. "I can't believe he came here."

"I suppose he must care more than you thought," Carley said.

Jean had laid down on the bed, and when the friends looked over, they could see that she had drifted to sleep.

"Are you really going to be all right sharing the room with him? After all you said, it sounds like it might be tough."

Laura smiled. "I didn't want to argue about it. I'll be okay, though. I've got through a lot today; I think I can get through sharing a room with my ex-husband."

Carley took hold of Laura's hand and gave it a squeeze.

"How do you feel about tomorrow?" Laura said, trying to change the subject.

"I think the police will work out what's going on. You were obviously acting in self-defence. Anyone would have done the same thing. They attacked me first…"

"We did kind of break into their house."

Carley considered this. "The end probably justifies the means or something. We came out of it with Jean here, so…"

Laura nodded in agreement. "I hope they see it that way."

When Laura and Jamie checked into their new room, she was pleased to see that he had indeed booked a twin. He threw his backpack onto the bed nearest to the door, leaving her the one next to the window.

They sat in silence for a couple of long minutes, with so much to say but so much uncertainty of how to begin to say it.

"Thanks for coming down here," Laura said, eventually. "I know I didn't give you the best welcome…"

"It wasn't the best of timing," Jamie smiled. "I didn't really expect that the next time I saw you, you'd be standing over the body of a man you'd knocked unconscious, to be honest."

"I'd like to say that I've changed," Laura managed to smile back, "But not quite *that* much."

"How did you get to us so quickly?" Laura asked. "I only told Mum where I was about an hour before you turned up."

"I was already in Cambridge," he admitted. Laura was sure that his face was turning red. "I talked to your Mum yesterday, and she told me all about this craziness. I had to come and check you were all right."

Laura's mouth widened. "Craziness?" she said. "Check I was all right?"

"It's a good job I did, isn't it?" Jamie said with bold indignance.

"As you said, Jamie, I was already standing over the body of a man that I'd knocked unconscious when you arrived. I really do appreciate you coming, but you were rather too late to do much to help."

She could feel herself becoming snappy with irritation. Was this what it had been like with Jamie? She remembered them being best friends, lovers, two people who should have always been together, but had drifted apart. Now, talking to him, she remembered how they had begun to wind each other up with the slightest comments.

There had been a bitter tension in their relationship that she hadn't even railed against when she was in it. This kind of behaviour had become so normal to her that only now, having lived without it for four months, could she recognise it for how malignant it was.

"Okay," Jamie said, holding up his hands like a criminal who had just been apprehended. "I didn't come here to fight. I still care about you, that's all. No matter what has happened between us, I care about you."

Laura swallowed and pressed her lips together tightly. She didn't want to argue either. The day had been extreme, and her emotions were obviously going to be on edge. There was no need to add to that by getting into something with her ex-husband.

"I care about you too. And really, thank you."

"Here," he said, throwing his phone onto her bed. "Now phone Catharine, and tell her what's happening."

"Maybe just the edited version," Laura smiled. "She worries more than you."

"Or maybe she just shows it better," Jamie said. He lay back on the bed and stretched out, crossing his legs at the ankles and staring at the ceiling.

Laura let her eyes wander over the man that she thought she would be spending her life with. He was a handsome guy, that was for sure. Seeing him there only a few feet from her stirred something within Laura, making her heart throb with the pain of their separation once more.

All it took to set her back on track was to think about the irritation he had also stirred within her. He was a good man, who had come here to help her, even if things hadn't panned out that way. For the first time, Laura's wish for their future changed. She had hoped, and even prayed, that something would happen to cause them to get back together. Now, she realised that having him as a friend, the way they used to be before their relationship soured, would be better for the both of them.

“Thanks, Jamie,” she said, before picking up his phone and calling Catharine.

CHAPTER THIRTY-FIVE

The tension over breakfast the following morning was intense. The three women picked at the eggs and bacon that they had reluctantly taken from the buffet, but no one had any real appetite. All they could think about, and talk about, was the forthcoming visit to the police station.

"If they were going to arrest you, they would have taken you last night," Jamie said, pushing a baked bean around his plate.

"Melanie and Gerrard could have made up any old story," Laura said. She had already rested her knife and fork across her plate, defeated.

"But you have a witness," Carley said. "Witnesses," she corrected, looking at Jean. "And surely what they have been doing to her… well, that will count for something. They can't get away with that."

"I don't want Gerry to be in trouble," Jean said. She looked as though she was constantly on the brink of tears, and it was understandable. "I know I had to get out, but I didn't want him to be in trouble.

He's not done anything wrong, not really. I just wanted to be out of that room."

Jamie looked across the table at the old lady and spoke with kind honesty. "You should never have been kept like that, Jean. I know he's your son and you love him very much, but what he did to you was wrong. It's not your fault. None of it is your fault."

Carley and Laura exchanged a fond look. Jamie had his moments.

"We spoke last night about Jean coming to Leeds to stay with me for a while, if the police are happy with that. I have a spare room, and nobody else to talk about books with all day," Carley said.

"Not in real life, anyway," Laura smiled. "You wouldn't be far away from me," she said to Jean, and then turned back to Carley to include her, too. "It would be good to see you both. If I'm not locked away somewhere."

Carley batted the idea away with a swipe of her hand. "Not going to happen."

"I'll drive us to the police station," Jamie offered. "That way, if you two get detained, at least I can take Jean somewhere..." He spoke in a deadpan voice, and when Laura and Carley looked at him with horrified expressions, laughed. "I'm joking! Nothing is going to happen."

"Sometimes you're just not funny, Jamie," Laura scolded.

Carley tried to hide her sniggers behind a napkin. "A little bit funny," she said.

They did decide to go to the station in Jamie's car, and much as Jamie suspected, everything went smoothly. Jamie told the police that he had only turned up after most of the excitement had happened, but he was still asked to tell the officers everything he had seen. The women were taken, one at a time, into the interview rooms to make their statements.

Laura couldn't stop her body from shaking as she sat across the Formica-topped table from two uniformed police officers. They switched on their recording device and started to ask questions. She had run through the explanation of how she had got the book and started the quest to find and help its owner so many times that it rolled neatly off her tongue by this point. The last week of her life had been flipped into disarray since she found the note, and she couldn't quite believe herself how much had happened.

"Can you tell me more about why you broke into Mr and Mrs Wexler's house?" the older of the two officers asked.

"We had gone all that way to help whoever sent the note. Carley worked out that there was someone else living there, and we were worried about them, about what was happening to them. We had to help them." She picked at the edge of the paper cup they had given her, trying to look at that rather than at their faces. Of course, she knew now that what she had done could be seen as stupid or irresponsible, but in the moment, she had acted on instinct. She had to help.

"And you didn't think, at that point, that phoning the police and letting us deal with it would be a better idea than breaking into the house and putting yourself in danger?"

Laura flushed with frustration. "We didn't do any damage to the house. The French doors were open, and we walked in."

"You seem to be missing the point," the other officer said. "You broke into the house and put yourself in danger rather than calling us. Why?"

Laura brought her eyes up to look at him. "You want to know why? Because when I phoned the police earlier this week to tell them about the note I found, the officer made me feel stupid. They didn't want to know." She waved her hands in exasperation. "So, I, we, Carley and I, we went ahead and tried to do what we could to help this person. Jean. We didn't know it was Jean then, but we knew it was someone, and we knew we had to do something. Yes, we should probably have phoned you then. Yes, we should probably not have *broken in* to the house, if you want to call it that, but we had to do something."

The officers exchanged a look, and the one who had seemed to be leading the questioning spoke. "Anything else you want to ask?" he said to his colleague.

"I think we have everything," he replied. Then he leaned forward and turned off the tape.

"Okay, Mrs Jacobs. Laura. What you did was remarkably stupid, and you ended up hurting two people. That those two people were, for all purposes, not very nice people is not the point. It's not your job to trail around the country, tracking people down and dishing out your own justice."

Laura trembled constantly as he spoke, and all she could do was nod.

"But we have also spoken to your friend, to Jean, and to the Wexlers. We've already built up a picture of what was happening there, and they needed to be stopped. If you hadn't stepped in, they would have no doubt continued doing what they were doing, and Jean Wexler would have continued to suffer."

Laura spoke, her voice quavering. "What *were* they doing? I mean, why were they keeping her there?"

The officers looked at each other again and the other spoke.

"We have conducted some initial enquiries, and it is already becoming clear that when Mr Charles Wexler, Jean's husband, passed away, the house..." He glanced at his notepad. "46, Radley

Street, was inherited solely by Jean Wexler. In fact, everything that Charles Wexler owned was inherited solely by Jean. He left nothing to his son."

Laura sat in silence as the officer continued.

"Charles was a wealthy man. He had worked hard and invested wisely. Gerrard Wexler, on the other hand, was almost flat broke."

"But the house is so…" It dawned on Laura as she spoke.

"It all belongs to Jean," the officer said. "Everything. The only way Gerrard and his wife can get a hold on it is to take control of her finances, and ultimately, of her decision-making ability. They moved into Radley Street soon after Charles Wexler passed away, and from what Jean has told us, she was thrilled to have them there. Melanie has played the part of the doting daughter-in-law to perfection. Gerrard, however, seems to have tired of waiting. He wanted the house, not his mother."

"So, he shut her away." Laura felt tears streaming down her cheeks. Poor, poor Jean. She had opened her home up to her son and his daughter, just as Catharine had taken her in. It was what you did as a mother. For Gerrard to take advantage of that love and kindness was unthinkable.

"So, he shut her away," the officer nodded. "And he has been using her bank account to finance his and Melanie's life. To quite a luxurious standard, as it turns out."

The three of them sat, taking in what had been said, letting the words settle.

"We will be taking action against Gerrard, and if we can gather enough evidence of Melanie's involvement against her, too. Jean paints a picture of a kind woman who has looked after her, despite having helped to keep her in that room. I know that you have a different impression of Melanie, but we need to investigate further. It's early days. I can tell you, though, that it's unlikely that you will face any charges on this occasion."

"But, Laura," the other officer said. "Stay out of trouble. Don't do anything like this again."

Laura let out a mammoth sigh, the tension flooding out of her body.

"No," she said. "Of course not."

As she stood to leave the room, the officer called her name. “Laura. There’s one more thing.”

Her heart sank. Had they changed their mind? Did she have to stay?

She turned to see the officer holding out his arm towards her. He had something shiny in his hand. Was he going to cuff her? Her legs felt weak for a moment.

“Your phone,” he said. “We got it back from the Wexlers’ safe.”

Laura rolled her eyes at her own stupidity and strolled over to take it.

“Stay out of trouble,” the other officer repeated.

“Believe me,” she said. “I will.”

It had been quite a week, but Laura had realised that thrillers were best experienced between the pages of a book, rather than being tangled up in them in real life. She didn’t want to experience the terror or excitement of the past week again unless she was reading about it.

EPILOGUE

Little did Laura think, when Gerrard had joked about interrupting Jean's book club, that such a meeting would become a reality.

Three months after *The Cambridge Business* as the women came to refer to it, Catharine and Laura were in the kitchen, baking a batch of lemon drizzle muffins in preparation for the inaugural meeting.

"How was work today?" Catharine asked, as she opened the oven to check on the fragrant cakes.

"So busy," Laura laughed. "But that's a good thing. There's a new apartment block just down from the stadium, and the commission on those flats is going to be amazing.

Catharine popped the door closed and leaned back against the counter.

"That's wonderful," she said. "Being busy is always better than being bored."

"They smell wonderful," Laura said.

"Well, lemon is Jean's favourite, so I had to make them," Catharine said with a smile. "Everything ready in there?"

Laura went around the living room one last time, plumping the cushions, putting the remote control onto her dad's side table and making sure the place looked spotless.

"Perfect," she said.

Bang on time, the doorbell rang.

"Go, go!" Catharine called from the kitchen. I'll get the kettle on.

Laura headed for the front door and opened it to greet her friends.

Carley met her with a beaming smile, always happy to see her best reading buddy. Jean lifted her nose to the air and sniffed twice, melodramatically.

"I smell lemon cake!" she said, not even trying to disguise her happiness.

"How are the lovely housemates?" Laura said, as they walked into the living room.

"Jean is helping me with my business now," Carley said. "I've got her designing my web page. Would you believe it?"

Laura would believe just about anything of Jean. She had shown herself to be a smart, independent woman over the time that Laura had been getting to know her. Far from the scared, trapped mouse that Laura had met back in Cambridge. With Carley's support and friendship, she was finding her way back to being herself again.

Catharine came in carrying a tray of tea. "You're going to have to wait until our break for the muffins," she said. "Nice to see you both." She put the tray down on the table and bent to hug both Carley and Jean.

The four women made themselves comfortable on the sofa and armchairs and settled their books onto their laps. Catharine and Laura rarely had time to watch daytime television anymore, now that Laura was back at work, and hardly found time to sit for longer than half an hour. The book club was a stark reminder of how they used to sit on this sofa and armchair for all those months when Laura needed to find *her* feet again. Catharine had helped Laura, and they had all between them helped Jean.

"Have you heard from Mel?" Catharine asked.

"She still phones me every day," Jean smiled. "I know she is terribly lonely without Gerry, but she's settling into her new place now. Maybe we can visit her soon."

Jean looked at Carley with such hope in her eyes that it seemed almost wrong that Laura shuddered at the thought of seeing Melanie again.

"Well, maybe," Carley said. "See what happens."

Jean nodded, satisfied, and Laura smiled at the plan that wasn't a plan. *See what happens* had got them that far, after all.

Laura's divorce with Jamie was going through, and they were finally spending time together as friends. She spoke to Carley and Jean regularly and saw them at least once a week. Being back at work was the best part, though. Something had changed, something positive, and more and more she found she could be Confident Laura without even trying.

What hadn't changed was her living arrangements. She was staying at home with her mum because she wanted to, not because she had to. She wanted to be with Catharine because she loved her and wanted to be with her, and because she knew the feeling was mutual. No matter what happened, she would never take their relationship for granted.

Jean opened her book and took the lead.

"Right then," she said. "What did we think of this one?"

Laura smiled contentedly. Even thrillers could have a happy ending.

Dear Reader

Thank you for choosing to read *The Book Swap*.

I hope you have enjoyed the book. If you liked it, please take a few minutes to leave a review on Goodreads, Amazon, or wherever you recommend books to others. Reviews help authors to find new readers and help readers to discover great books.

If you would like to read more of my books, please visit my website, jerowney.com where you can find links to all of my books. You can also sign up to my mailing list for a free novel and updates on all my future books.

Best wishes
J.E. Rowney

Lightning Source UK Ltd.
Milton Keynes UK
UKHW040923290722
406557UK00001B/18

9 781739 68992